THE ART OF MURDER

Sean Mallon Book 1

RICK WOOD

Blood Splatter Press

Rick Wood

Rick Wood is a British writer born in Cheltenham.

His love for writing came at an early age, as did his battle with mental health. After defeating his demons, he grew up and became a stand-up comedian, then a drama and English teacher, before giving it all up to become a full-time author.

He now lives in Loughborough, where he divides his time between watching horror, reading horror, and writing horror.

Also By Rick Wood

The Sensitives
The Sensitives
My Exorcism Killed Me
Close to Death
Demon's Daughter
Questions for the Devil
Repent
The Resurgence
Until the End

Blood Splatter Books
Psycho B*tches
Shutter House
This Book is Full of Bodies
Home Invasion

Cia Rose
After the Devil Has Won
After the End Has Begun
After the Living Have Lost
After the Dead Have Decayed

The Edward King Series
I Have the Sight
Descendant of Hell
An Exorcist Possessed
Blood of Hope
The World Ends Tonight

Anthologies
Twelve Days of Christmas Horror
Twelve Days of Christmas Horror Volume 2
Roses Are Red So Is Your Blood

Standalones
When Liberty Dies
The Death Club

Sean Mallon
The Art of Murder
Redemption of the Hopeless

Chronicles of the Infected
Zombie Attack
Zombie Defence
Zombie World

Non-Fiction
How to Write an Awesome Novel
The Writer's Room

Rick also publishes thrillers under the pseudonym Ed Grace…
Jay Sullivan
Assassin Down
Kill Them Quickly
The Bars That Hold Me
A Deadly Weapon

© Copyright Rick Wood 2016

Edited by The Writers' Workshop

Copy Edited by Lee Ann at FirstEditing.com

Cover Design by bloodsplatterpress.com

Rick Wood Publishing

Chapter One

SEAN MALLON HAD no idea what it was like to take a life.

Until he did.

It was easier than he expected. The choice was the suspect or Sean, and when the choice was so simple, the knife slid in like butter.

It was Sean's reflection that haunted him. The rippled imitation of his face in the puddle beside his feet.

He could still feel the thick blood sliding through his fingers.

He could still see the eyes of horror on his opponent's face.

The press somehow knew before his colleagues had. They swarmed around the door like locusts, flooding the front garden like a potent plague.

They labelled Sean a police hero. They reported that he had single-handedly raided a sex offender's house, defending himself as his life was threatened, killing in self-defence to free the children this disgusting man had tormented for so long.

None of them knew he had gone against specific orders.

None of them were able to report that this defiance left him suspended and an outcast to the officers he had let down in doing so.

It was Sean's word against a criminal's. A testimony no one could argue with. This wasn't the way they liked to play it.

His fame was short-lived. The praise vanished and the attention faded away.

The psychological evaluations persisted.

The therapists, the drugs, the pushing people away; these things didn't leave so easily.

Sean stood in that doorway every day of his life. Every time he closed his eyes, he would be slouched over the warm, pale corpse, looking into those dead eyes, his hands dripping with dark-red gunk.

He saw the scene as he fumbled onto the porch, hollering with shame. The cheers of the neighbours, the clamouring of the press, the flashing of the cameras; they slowed down, turning into distortions and streaks blurring his vision.

His detective superintendent's voice screaming at Constables turned to ringing in Sean's ears. Numerous detective constables dragged him out of the limelight, tearing him away, attempting to isolate him from the outside world.

His hands.

The blood.

It was so warm.

Those fingers, blood trickling between them, life falling away.

He fell to his knees as the officers dragged him away from the public eye.

No one had ever told Sean what it would be like to take a life; he'd never had that training session. No one told Sean about the hypocrisy of his fame. He had already been worshipped for famously putting away a serial killer over an eight-month operation.

Now, he was the killer.

He had not wanted to do it.

They hailed him as a hero. They begged him to stay.

He packed his desk and never looked back.

ONE YEAR LATER

Chapter Two

LET me tell you what it's like to die.

It's the final moments of a battery.

It's the draining power, ripping control away from you.

It's the dilation of a pupil when you're close to someone you love.

It's the satisfaction of a tiger as it pounces upon a deer.

It's the end of a sad movie that you thought would never end.

Shelley didn't know what it was like to die when she groaned, leant over, and hit snooze on her alarm. She didn't know how fleeting the pain would be. No, her thoughts were on how she was going to get through another twelve-hour shift without getting sexually harassed as she pulled up her demeaning skirt and attached her stained apron.

As she tucked her pad into her breast pocket, she looked herself in the mirror. A twenty-five-year-old mother of three, desperately working double shifts to keep her children clothed and fed.

Someday I'll leave this town, she told herself, bumbling out the front door, her children's breakfast stained upon her white blouse. *Someday I'll make a better life.*

Half-way through her double shift and her composure was breaking.

"What you doing later?" one manky bloke in a vest had asked her.

"You should smile more, doll," some lad showing off to his mates had claimed, his wide-open mouth revealing a half-eaten sausage sandwich. He high-fived his mates as she meandered away with her head dropped.

"Come sit on my lap," was a familiar request she had grown used to. Though on this particular shift, it was followed by a greasy hand grabbing a large chunk of her backside.

She bumbled into the kitchen with her hands over her face. As she leant against the dishwasher, about to tell her best friend about her desire to slap the hell out of the chauvinist pig in the dining area, she paused as she looked to the door.

An odd-looking gentleman leisurely strolled into the café, sitting particularly and precisely at a table beside the window. He was short, with glasses taking up most of his face and his hair was parted without a strand out of place. He wore loose brown trousers and braces over a checked shirt, accompanied by a tweed bowtie.

The man never stopped smiling.

Shelley watched with an intense interest as he requested a coffee with three sugars and thanked his waitress with thorough politeness.

As soon as the coffee was placed before him, he took a deep, clean sip, following by an elongated, "Aaah."

Shelley's best friend came to her side and joked "I bet he's a virgin. He looks so weird."

"Guys, come on, we don't know him," Shelley responded, still curious about this man's strange demeanour.

As she continued her shift, she kept a vague focus on him, intrigued by his whole weird appearance. For an hour, he barely moved. His hands lay flat on the table, his arms resting beside his mug, symmetrically placed over his open legs. He slurped each sip of his coffee with excessive volume, requesting another one every twenty minutes like clockwork.

Shelley filled up his eighth cup. Smiling at him in her typical friendly manner, she asked, "You meeting someone today, hon?"

His eyes looked her up and down, slowly, leering at her without subtlety. He looked like a lion taking in his prey. He breathed in deeply through his nose, closing his eyes, receiving her scent. He paused. Enjoyed it.

A shiver ran down Shelley's spine. This was seriously creeping her out.

"I sure am," he replied, peering at her name tag for her name. "… Shelley." A grin spread from cheek to cheek. "But I only just this minute realised who it was I was waiting for."

Her breath stuck in her throat.

He abruptly ascended to his feet. His hand took the back of her hair in his fist, pulling it tightly, using all the force of his triceps to slam her face through the table.

Terrified shrieks resounded around the café. Numerous customers jumped out of their seats and backed up against the walls.

Blood trickled down Shelley's broken nose and a couple of teeth dropped to the floor like pins. She was too dizzy to comprehend what was happening. Her eyes kept a hazy awareness as her head was lifted up again and smashed upon the table once more.

The entire café flooded out the door among screams of

shock and fear. Not a soul even attempted to stop the man murdering a woman in the middle of a busy café.

Once he had finished killing her, the man lifted her blouse drenched with red, and wrote his message upon her chest.

Chapter Three

SEAN RUED the day he agreed to this shit. He'd dreamt of being a doctor. Still, it was better than a security guard. That could wait until retirement.

It was 5.00 a.m. The time of the morning most thirty-year-old men would be waking next to their beautiful wives. They would ungratefully smack snooze on their alarm, maybe turn and grin at the woman next to them. They would think about how much they wished they didn't have to go to work, irritated about having to sit on their arse all day, doing bugger all.

Sean wasn't like that person at all.

Sean spent his nights following cheating arseholes for rich clients. The vision of a private investigator (a private investigator, not a private detective, as he would constantly remind people) – was that you would spend action-filled nights hunting murderers and solving impossible cases.

Truth is, it was far less glamorous. But Sean liked that.

The less attention he brought himself, the better. He hadn't enjoyed his time in the public eye, and was happy not to have to relive it. The quiet life suited him.

This night was typical of most nights; following potential cheating husbands and wives around for suspicious spouses with a ridiculous, bottomless supply of money. Almost every time he would end up confirming that these husbands and wives were in fact cheating, and would supply the evidence he needed.

The police did have its benefits, mind. He used to love the respect he would get through being the senior investigating officer and coordinating an investigation to solve impossible murders. The exciting moment when you finally send someone down for a killing they were adamant they would get away with. He had earnt his status as 'The Psychopath Hunter' – a name that made him blush, but he was secretly pleased with.

He got far more credit than supplying pictures of some cheating whore with a cock in her mouth.

His mind wandered back to his final case, the sex offender, the house he raided alone.

Blood consumed his hand.

He knew it wasn't there, but he saw it nonetheless.

The lifeless, pale face of a dead pervert gaped up at him from beneath his feet.

Those familiar feelings returned.

That foreboding, sinister, overwhelming trepidation in his gut as the thought that he had just taken a life disbursed through the forefront of his mind.

Stop it, Sean, for fuck's sake.

He snapped himself back to reality. Focussed on the man he was watching screw his secretary through the crack in the curtains of a hotel room window.

He withdrew a packet of paroxetine and a pot of sertraline. He gazed at his hand as he popped one of each into his palm.

Taking antidepressants was shit. But, if the alternative

was therapy, he'd do it. Talking to some prick who sat there writing down everything he said, judging him with their hypocritical, defunct, shitty eyes, only incensed him further.

So here I am. From legend to this.

He tormented his mind with what could have been, then convinced himself he wasn't that good a policeman anyway. Arresting people made him feel like a hypocrite; he wasn't the angelic policeman his mother used to tell everyone he was.

Finally, Sean took the photographs that this creep's wife was paying £1,000 each for and packed up his equipment.

As he breathed in the fresh night air, he decided he would walk back to the office. There was no one else around, and he enjoyed silent, moonlit walks. He worked at night, as this was how he liked it. Peaceful. Tranquil.

He stopped by the liquor store and bought a few cans of lager with a rolled-up note that he found crumpled in his back pocket. He was halfway through the first can by the time he arrived at the desk outside his office doors ten minutes later.

As he stepped forward, his apprentice, Jack, came trotting toward him.

"I'm so sorry, Sean, he wouldn't leave, I'm so sorry-"

Sean barged past Jack, bursting through the door to his office, slamming the door in Jack's face.

Sean let out a frustrated sigh and shook his head in annoyance. August Daniels looked back at Sean with a knowing smirk etched across his face.

Sean was half-drunk, half-shaven and struggling to go half an hour without a graphic flashback; this was not the state Sean wanted his former colleague to see him in.

"It's good to see you, Sean," August told him. He sat back in Sean's office chair, his hands resting on his lap and his foot upon his knee. He wore a shirt and tie, with hair carefully parted with gel; which looked far tidier than Sean's hair style of 'however I got up this morning.'

"Get out my seat," Sean demanded.

August obliged.

As Sean put his jacket over his chair, August instead leant against the desk. He watched Sean, seemingly bemused.

"So what, you just come here to stare at me like a goat?" Sean snapped. He instantly regretted comparing him to a goat as he realised it made little sense. Ah well. His mind didn't work as fast as it used to.

"So this is what the legendary psychopath hunter does now, then? Takes pictures of adulterous husbands. Really?"

Sean ignored him.

"So how's your daughter?"

"I wouldn't know, August."

Sean sat still, temporarily closing his eyes, attempting to remain calm. His foot tapped the floor, his hands clasped and his heart beat a little faster. He was trying.

"What do you want?"

"I need you to come back."

"I'm not coming back." Sean vigorously shook his head, frantically tidying his desk in an attempt to look nonchalant.

"I understand what happened–"

"You clearly do not!"

"I do understand. If I killed a man, then–"

"Get out!" Sean screamed, charging over to the door and opening it, staring at August with determined eyes.

"Okay, okay," August spoke softly, edging toward the door with no real intention of leaving. "But won't you at least hear the case?"

"Not interested."

Sean stormed away from the door, leaving it open for August, retaking his desk chair and rearranging his stationery, the whole time keeping his eyes down and away from his old friend.

"Sean."

"What?"

August sighed, peering around the office. There were no headlines, no trophies, no memories. Just clutter.

Except for one solitary picture of Sean's daughter.

August closed his eyes and dropped his head. It was going to take a full explanation to convince Sean.

"You helped the Birmingham Met catch the most prolific serial killer of our generation. You have legendary status, not just there, but… what happened, happened. It sucks. But now there is another serial killer that we are struggling with and… he's too clever. We need someone with experience and expertise in this area. No one else in the department has even come close to anything like a serial killer or a psychopath."

Sean chewed on the end of his pen as he leant back in his chair. He considered the proposition. Then he remembered why he left.

I can't keep seeing blood on my hands.

"I don't know August…"

"Please, Sean. People are dying. Children – are dying."

Sean huffed. He leant forward and ran his hands through his hair.

"It's not fair that you are doing this to me."

"I know."

He gave August a faint nod. "This is temporary. I see the body, give you my assessment, then we're done."

"Okay."

"So where is this serial killer?"

"Gloucestershire."

Chapter Four

SEAN FLINCHED at the smell of manure and the sight of fields surrounding the country road to Gloucester.

Sean was a city man, through and through. He'd been stationed temporarily in a countryside town many years ago, and found he spent most of his time chasing lost sheep. He'd longed for the action of the city, and despised the small-town attitudes of the locals.

He gave a big sigh as August pulled up outside a cheap café. It stank like a mixture of cannabis and bins. Sean rolled his eyes and rubbed his sinus. This is not where he wanted to be.

August led Sean and Jack to the crime scene. They were halted outside and made to sign in. Even the feel of the pen in his hand, producing his signature in the correct box, conjured up feelings he'd buried deep down.

The body of a woman lay in the middle of surrounding yellow tape, the side of her face engulfing the floor, teeth missing and dried blood so crusted that it kept her eyes stuck wide open. Her rear end was stuck in the air, her knees and face propping her up, with help from the stiffening that a body endures in death.

Sean observed the body for a few seconds before flinching his eyes away. His face screwed up.

He used to be so used to the sight of a dead body, but it was like it was all new again. He willed himself to overcome his trepidation. Bracing himself, his eyes returned to the body again.

The cause of death was obvious; trauma to the head. Or, as Sean saw it, repeated bashing of head on table.

Blood. Soaking through Sean's hands.

It's just in my mind.

He closed his eyes and willed the thoughts away. He couldn't. Everything became red. Then he saw another corpse. A corpse he had once created...

Shut up. It's not real.

He shoved his hand into his inside pocket and produced his medication in a rapid movement. He popped a few pills of paroxetine, swallowing them straight down without any water.

Why can't I just go a day with having a fucking breakdown?

Burying the images deep in the back of his mind, he focussed on August. August informed that this woman was both the sixth and the eldest victim.

Six? All younger than mid-twenties? Sean fought familiar feelings of sickness. His stomach churned. How had he ever been used to this job?

Upon Sean's request, August gave him more specific detail. Her name was Shelley Dale; a waitress, mother of three, twenty-five-years-old. The killer had supposedly sat in plain sight for over an hour before unexpectedly beating her head against the table and simply strolling out. Apparently, no one did a damn thing to stop him leaving.

A murderer in plain sight and no one bothered to restrain him. They could have ended the case right then and there. What a society we live in.

"Who's the senior investigating officer? Or detective superintendent?" Sean requested.

"Me," August boasted. Sean scoffed. Last time they worked together August failed his Inspector exam. How times change.

"Do we have a murder incident room set up?"

"With a station for each victim."

"CCTV?"

"Nada." The CCTV had caught nothing. According to the café's manager, it didn't even take videos, just a black-and-white picture every sixty seconds.

CCTV a century old. Wonderful.

The images CCTV had produced displayed a man who, whilst elaborately dressed, stared ahead the entire time. Not once did he raise his head long enough for a clean shot of his face to be taken. Even though he dressed with some originality, he had no clearly identifiable marks or features. Sean had his build and approximate height, along with numerous witness descriptions of "odd-looking." Not much of a bloody help.

Once the suspect left the diner, he'd gotten into a car with a license plate that, according to their system, doesn't exist. Being in 'the country' there were no more cameras along the subsequent country roads and they had not clocked his license plate on any cameras anywhere else.

Bluntly put, they had nothing in the way of tracking him, and had all their hope in what they found via the crime scene.

More in-depth descriptions from waitresses and customers were similar. Neatly dressed, although a little child-like, parted hair, no facial hair, and a creepy smile. *We are looking for a creepy smile, ladies and gentlemen.*

He gazed at the body. He needed a stiff drink. His mind wandered to whether he'd be able to afford the good whiskey from the shop later.

Jack, his far younger and inexperienced apprentice, took Sean's side. Jack was much scrawnier than Sean's well-built exterior. Sean's standard appearance was a tight white shirt under a leather jacket, showing off what little muscle he had left. He hadn't had a gym membership for almost two years and his liver must be almost destroyed by now, yet he still had some toned muscles that he was proud to show off. Jack, on the other hand, suited his shorter exterior with baggier clothing. Everyone could see from the way Jack looked at his partner he was in awe of the track record Sean had. Sean knew this, which was why he liked having him around.

"Any ideas, boss?" Jack peered up at Sean.

Sean grunted. He knew he should reply properly; but the less he said, the more the kid hung on his every word. His hair was scruffy and he had a poor attempt at a moustache under his lip. He wrote all his notes down in a small pad containing a photo of his daughter underneath the cover. The only piece of information Sean knew about Jack was how much he loved his daughter; other than that, Sean would be at a loss to tell you anything about him.

"Let's see what the Scenes of Crime Officers have to say. Find out if the Police Search Team have been in yet." Upon Sean's command, Jack instantly sought out the SOCO and the PST teams for their information, leaving Sean a chance to sneak a few sips of Jack Daniels from his pocket. He needed it.

As Sean enjoyed the moment of bliss that occurs after the first sip of whiskey in a dry throat, he took out his wallet. Inside was a picture of a young girl with blond hair.

"I miss you…" he whispered. He'd give anything to see his daughter's face again. How he could use her magic smile right now. The simple act of reading a book with his daughter on his lap used to make all the morbidity of his job fade away.

He visited the Murder Incident Room with August and looked over what they had already. For each crime scene it was the same; an aerial view of the suspect with no real shot of his face, a murder in the middle of nowhere with little in the way of tracking him, and a different car each time that supposedly didn't exist. DNA was always the same, but didn't belong to anyone in their system. They had tyre tracks from forensics, which led them to a large tyre manufacturer with many clients and, ultimately, a dead end.

Whilst Sean surveyed the evidence, he was aware of all the eyes glued on him. The officers looked to him like he was some kind of genius. Since catching a serial killer, he had gained a status he didn't feel he had earned. He felt more at home being branded as 'lucky' than 'wise.'

He racked his brains with them until the early hours of the morning. He went over their levels of enquiry that had gone dead, to find nothing new.

It only confirmed to Sean what use he believed he would be.

Finally, a light with a tint of orange began to grow in the sky, signalling the night being over and morning arriving. He retired to his hotel room for a few hours of peace.

Chapter Five

AS SEAN ARRIVED in the hotel room, the image of Shelley's body fresh at the forefront of his mind, he dumped his jacket on the floor and took out a bottle of whiskey. No matter how strenuously he fought, he couldn't shake the sight away.

Climbing onto his bed, he distracted himself by sifting through the office mail Jack had dropped off.

Sean ignored envelope after envelope that looked like bills. Eventually, he was pleasantly surprised by a handwritten letter. He dumped the rest in the bin and opened it.

DEAR MR MALLON,

RE: Case Number 256

Thank you for your letter of information regarding the denial of seeing your daughter. We understand this is a complicated case and we are working closely with your ex-partner to come to a resolution.

As it stands, your ex-partner has refused to allow you any custody or visitation rights.

If you would like to follow this with further legal action, we suggest that you consult your attorney.

. . .

HE STOPPED READING with a grimace at the paper and scrunched it up in his hands. He hurled it toward the bin, missing completely.

His daughter would be twelve now. She would be far taller than the six-year-old he remembered taking to the beach and teaching how to ride a bike. What he wouldn't give to see her again. He would give up everything, walk one-thousand miles, even run butt-naked through the streets of Birmingham City Centre, if only it meant he could have one more minute with his daughter.

After filling up his tumbler with an excessive amount of whiskey, he flicked on the lamp and lay down, pulling a large book from his bag. It was his old scrapbook; he never travelled without it. The pages were covered. Pictures and newspaper clippings of killers caught and abusers defeated, interspersed with memories of his daughter.

On the last page was Sean's final victory; a picture of him leaving the house of a prolific sex offender, his hands drenched with blood. The report beneath read:

HERO POLICE OFFICER SEAN MALLON, pictured above, today completed his role as senior investigative officer in the case of Alexander Shirlov, a prolific paedophile. Shirlov had been holding three young boys in his basement for the purpose of creating child pornography, who were all freed by Mallon upon his entry to Shirlov's property.

After fending off an attack by the child rapist, Mallon ended up having to use ultimate force.

Shirlov had been responsible for the abduction and sexual assault of more than eight boys and four girls, including being a suspect in the murder of two of said girls.

After single-handedly taking down Shirlov, Mallon's exit of the house was met with rapturous applause. "Rightly so," said neighbour Mildred Hans. "That man had tortured those children. Sean Mallon did a heroic thing."

IT WAS SUPPOSED to make him proud. It was supposed to be an achievement. But it only made him feel like a fraud.

His eyes fixed on this article like he was in a trance. It was the only thing he had that didn't highlight how much of a loser he was. There was no woman in his bedroom, no girlfriend's make-up left in the bathroom and no second place laid at his table.

Before he turned out the light and tucked himself under the duvet, he undertook his nightly routine. Pulling his mini-safe out of the suitcase beside his bed, he twisted the dial to ensure its security was intact.

Still locked. Still safe.

He breathed a sigh of relief. Although he checked this drawer's security every day, he still felt relieved to ensure it was secure. He was reassured that what lay inside of it remained secret.

No one could ever see the contents of that safe.

Five glasses of whiskey later, Sean still lay in bed, refusing to go to sleep and let the images of Shelley Dalel's body plague his unconscious. As he filled up another glass, his procrastination led him into a folder on his phone entitled "Charlotte." In there, he found pictures of him and his daughter: sitting on his lap reading, running through the park, playing with Barbies; dozens of pictures with dozens of memories. He smiled as a tear fell from his eye.

"Goodnight, sweetheart," he whispered to the phone, placing it on the bedside table.

As he finally drifted off to sleep, his unconscious still

tortured him. Images of a knife gripped in his hand, slicing the neck beneath Alexander Shirlov's gaping face.

At one point he woke up with a jolt, screaming and staring at his hands.

He went back to sleep, only to see himself furiously stabbing once more.

Chapter Six

THE FAMILIAR SOUND of his iPhone ringtone repeated for an age before it eventually woke Sean up. He stirred, lifting his head and knocking a tumbler glass off the bed and along the floor. He groggily rubbed his face and lifted his phone in front of his eyes, slowly adjusting its distance from his eyes so he could read who the caller was.

"What?" he barked into the receiver.

"Sean, where have you been?" came the alert voice of some female officer he didn't recognise. "We need you to come to the Dog and Hound in town centre, now."

"Bit early for a pint, ennit?" Sean chuckled to himself, though he did contemplate how nice an early morning beer would be.

"No, there has been another murder. And it has your name on it."

Sean assumed they meant figuratively – as in, "that beer has your name on it." Glancing at the clock that read 9.30a.m., he wondered whether he could find some way out of having to go look at another corpse. The front of his head was pounding and his mouth was dry. He never used to endure this kind of hangover when he was younger.

"Yeah, okay, let me just—"

"No, Sean. You don't get it. This murder literally has your name written on it."

"How does it have my name on it? What, it's written in blood?" he mused.

A sigh of hesitation came through the phone. "We think you'd better see it yourself. Just hurry up and get here." The call ended.

Sean leant back and rubbed his eyes. He squinted at the sun light attacking him through the window. Leaning up, he registered the mess of whiskey stains on the bed sheet. Shaking his head with a big sigh, he clambered through the mess on the floor, grabbed his jacket and left.

FIFTEEN MINUTES LATER, Sean pulled up outside the Dog and Hound. It was a typical British pub, in an old building. He assumed it was family owned; the kind of pub where the barman knew the regulars by name and drink.

He had only been out of his car for seconds when Jack came frantically scurrying up to him, gesticulating all over the place.

"Sean, you've got to see this. No one has touched the body, we've all been waiting for you. We just... don't understand."

This kid has a lot to learn.

Sean recalled being like Jack once. It must have been many years ago. Before he became jaded and cynical. Before his drinking turned from 'youthful rebellion' to 'sad old git.'

August greeted Sean cautiously, Sean feeling as if there was a big secret he wasn't in on. Placing a white suit on to match the Scenes of Crime Officers, he signed in and entered the crime scene through the entry point; a small path created through the side of the doorway guarded by a constable.

As Sean entered the pub, he dropped to his knees.

What he beheld paralysed him. His jaw dropped, his throat closed up and his gut churned into knots.

Against the wall of the pub was a young girl – around nine or ten, by Sean's guess – nailed to the wall by the palm of her hands. Her head was dropped forward, covering a deep wound across her neck, congealed with dried blood. The killer hadn't even given her the dignity of clothes.

Across her naked torso, the words were written in what looked like red permanent marker:

HAVE YOU RECEIVED MY MESSAGES, Sean?

SEAN COULDN'T MOVE. His hands concealed his mouth, his eyes cemented on the body of a poor child who had been demeaned and tortured. He had seen some sick, repulsive remains in his time, including young girls and the horrific experiences psychopaths had made them endure. Nothing like the humiliating mess pinned to the wall of this pub. This was vile, and sadistic in the extreme.

Everything turned black and white. A red filter, as if being placed in front of a camera lens, came travelling vertically down his vision.

Self-hatred circled his mind. His rejection of his instincts confused him. Breathing quickened pace, eyelids shivered, palms became sweaty.

Every other officer on the scene; August, the Scenes of Crime Officers, constables guarding passages, detective constables gathering testimonies; they froze and turned to Sean. They couldn't tear their eyes away from him. Everyone was tense.

His breathing amplified to such an enhanced pace his head became faint and his cranium pounded. As if having an extreme head rush, multi-coloured streaks crossed in front of him. His heart boomed against his ribs like a car over a succession of speed bumps.

Sean burst out of the crime scene, disregarding the entry point, falling to his knees on the cement outside. He instantly threw up a potent mouthful of vomit, consisting mostly of blood and whiskey. His hands and feet quivered uncontrollably and his breathing briskly heightened as he struggled to control his thoughts.

Red. Blood red.

Seeping through his fingers.

Shirlov's throat cut.

His hands taking a life.

He pawed frantically for the pills in his pocket, urgently unscrewing the lid, bypassing his hands and pouring sertraline straight into his mouth. Choking on the pills, he swallowed them and immediately calmed.

How does this killer know me? I've been here for half a day; how does he know I am here? Who is this bastard?

"I can't do this… I can't do this…"

August came to his side and placed a hand on Sean's back. He studied Sean and, once he was sure Sean was back in control, he led him to a bench.

August barked at the gaping officers to stop staring and get on with their jobs, and they quickly scurried away.

"Her name was Felicia Howard," August testified. "Nine years and ten months. She was reported missing by her parents yesterday afternoon, when they went to pick her up from school but she wasn't there."

Sean closed his eyes. He would give anything to be back outside a window to a dodgy hotel room, taking pictures of a cheating husband for extortionate amounts of money.

"Is this the real reason you wanted me? Not because of my expertise, because my fucking name has been on the bodies?"

August glanced uncomfortably to the floor, then back to Sean

"Yes, it was. Both reasons, really. We need your expertise. But we also need to know why he's targeting you."

"I've made enemies with many psychopaths."

"But you've caught all those psychopaths. Where would this person's grudge come from?"

Sean closed his eyes and pretended he was somewhere else. A beach, maybe. With his daughter. Building sand castles and paddling in the sea.

These thoughts faded into his bloody hands once more, intruding on his thoughts. He opened his eyes with a start, forcing the bad thoughts away.

If I'm going to do this, I'm going to have to do this properly...

"Was she marked present at her school?"

"For the morning, yes. After her lunch break, no one had any sight of her."

"Jack, get over here." Jack came scurrying up to Sean. "I want you to contact her school, get all CCTV of an hour before their lunch break, to an hour after lunch. I want detective constables interviewing teachers. I want detective constables interviewing students. I want to know the girl's mental state, her actions, everything that can give us a picture up to her disappearing. Tell the headmaster to look at the CCTV with you and screenshot any adult or child he does not recognise or looks suspicious."

Jack speedily noted down the instructions on his pad before scarpering off like an obedient dog.

"Do you think I'm the best person to be on this case, with this come to light?"

"Sean, I think you're the *only* guy who should be on this case. If the killer is taunting you, you need to make your presence here known. If you're the bait, let's… hook him in, and reel him in."

Sean returned to the body, fixating on it, without removing his eyes. He placed his hands in his pockets.

Have you received my messages Sean?

What was he missing? How did the killer know his name?

"August?"

"Yeah?"

"I need to see the other messages."

Chapter Seven

SEAN STOOD STRAIGHT AND TALL, his arms folded, watching the activity of the Murder Incident Room. Around him were officers sifting through CCTV footage and witness testimony, desperately trying to find something they could use.

Upon the wall were five images of different bodies in various states, each displaying a different message. The first two were teenage girls, the third a young boy, the fourth a young girl and the fifth, Shelley Dalel. This time, Sean could see what was written underneath Shelley Dalel's blouse.

Each message mentioned Sean by name.

Come out and play Sean.
Sean where are you?
Will you save them now Sean?
Sean is a coward.

"How do we know it's definitely me and not another Sean?"

August pointed to the words written on the chest of Shelley Dalel.

Sean Mallon the psychopath hunter, where are you?
"Oh."

A detective constable sauntered up behind them with a few sheets of paper. Sean saw on her badge that her name was DC Elizabeth Hurks.

"This is the testimony from the witnesses from each crime scene."

"They won't be any good."

Elizabeth recoiled, frowning. "Why not?"

Sean sighed and stroked his chin. He lost patience when having to explain thinking to a rookie. Still, August looked interested in his take on the situation.

"This guy is all about voyeurism, he wants to be seen."

"Then won't what people see be useful?"

"They only see what the killer wants them to. Same way he only lets us see on CCTV what he wants us to see. He lets us see a car that we can't pick up driving away; he's taunting us. He lets us see the aerial view of his head; he's taunting us. It's the same with witness testimony. Whatever they see will just be part of his taunt."

Elizabeth stood back and folded her arms, sticking out her lip. In his mind, Sean likened her to a petulant child.

"What do you suggest?" August prompted.

"The victims. Let's find out if he's taunting us with them. Find a correlation. I'll go to the primary school with Jack. Send DCs out to all crime scenes, study all photos, find out if there is a pattern in the victims that he's using to taunt us. That could help us find the next victim."

Sean grabbed his coat and left the room, leaving them with his final statement. "Catch the next victim, we catch the killer."

"SHE WAS SUCH A LOVELY CHILD," sobbed Mrs Simons, her tears magnified behind her gigantic, round glasses. "I don't know whatever could come over someone to do such a thing."

Sean sat back and exhaled. He was growing tired. He had spent most of his day sitting with family liaison officers and psychiatrists, trying to help the teachers and students recall anything relevant. They needed to catch a killer, not hug a bunch of teachers.

She looked like a primary school teacher would if they were in a cartoon. She wore a long, green, baggy skirt, with a flowery blouse covered by a woolly cardigan. Her hair was long and tied back, and her glasses were big and circular. She looked young, yet old for her age. Sean would probably guess late 20s. She looked to Sean like the kind of hippy who would enjoy finger painting with nine-year-olds all day.

"Mrs Simons, I understand you are upset, but I need you to focus if we are to catch the killer."

"Right. Sorry." She wiped her tears away with a brown, grotesque-looking hanky, tucking it inside of her sleeve. She gathered herself and appeared to make a concerted effort to hold her emotions back.

"What kind of girl would you say she was?"

She pondered this for a few moments. "She was a very bubbly girl, very infectious personality, everyone loved her. She would always bring me flowers, even when she wasn't allowed to pick them. She was kind, caring; she was so, so nice. It's so sad."

Sean scribbled in his notepad. For all her babbling, he managed to summarise what she said as 'nice girl.'

"And you saw her before she went out to play for lunch?"

"Yes, I did. So sad…"

"How would you describe her mental state before she left?"

"Erm…. There was nothing different, not obviously, anyway. She had just finished doing an art project where she used wax crayons to make a picture of a plant. It looked so nice that I gave her a star – that's how we reward children here. She was smiling and happy about it before she left to go play in the playground."

"Any one leave the classroom with her?"

"No… I think she was alone."

Sean managed to summarise in his notes 'left happy, alone.'

"And when was it you noticed that she wasn't there?"

"We didn't. I mean, we change classes for maths in the afternoon. I guess we all just assumed she was in the other class. It wasn't until her parents came…." She started crying again, snorting into her hanky. "Oh God, I feel so responsible!"

Sean couldn't tell her she wasn't. It was stupid of her to not be accountable for the whereabouts of a child in her care.

"Thank you, Mrs Simons. I appreciate it."

Sean left and re-joined Jack in a classroom the school had vacated for their place of operation. They had spent all day talking to these people and he was, honestly, exhausted.

"Did you find anyone who looked like him on the CCTV?"

"No," replied his lapdog.

"Looked at all of it?"

"Sat there for six hours looking at all different angles, didn't take our eyes off the screen once. She left for lunch, got caught up in a group of children, was nowhere to be seen after that. No unrecognised people. Whoever did this… they were good."

Sean hated the idea of complimenting a killer, but Jack was right; the killer was taunting them with every action they took. The killer knew who Sean was, they knew how to take a child in plain sight, and they knew how to kill a woman in front of a whole café and not be noticed beforehand. They were up against it and Sean knew it.

"Has anyone interviewed the parents?"

Jack shook his head. Sean checked his watch and noticed that it was approaching 11.30 p.m. He was already yawning.

"I'm going to look at the Scenes of Crime Officers' report in my hotel," Sean announced. "You go interview the parents. Record it and send me the audio. I'll tell August to keep officers at the station going over all possible correlations and similarities. He can call us when we have something. There's nothing more we can do today."

Jack nodded and departed.

Sean made his way back to the hotel with the forensic report, alone.

THE SHRILL SHRIEKING of Sean's room landline echoed around the walls.

He stirred, turning over and slightly opening one eye. A blurry 4.40 am came into view. He rolled onto his back and let out a long groan. What would happen if he chose not to answer it?

The noise persisted. Why didn't they call him on his mobile? If he was honest with himself, Sean wasn't even sure he knew the room had a landline.

He sat up in bed. Whoever this dick-head was, they weren't going away. Without being completely conscious of what he was doing, he landed his feet on the floorboards that felt like ice. He never had the heating on; there wasn't much point if he was hardly there.

"Fuck," he exclaimed as he stepped on an empty whiskey glass, sending it rolling across the room. It landed in a shadow where it clinked with some other glass.

He lifted the phone to his ear and slumped down against the wall, rubbing his eyes. "What?" he prompted, hoping whoever was calling would recognise the displeasure in his voice.

No response. Sean decided that if this was a prank phone call, he would endeavour to use police resources to track down whoever the joker was. Once he'd had a lie in, of course.

"Is there anyone there?" he sang out with agitation.

The faint sound of low-pitched chuckling came through the receiver.

"Think this is funny, do you?"

"I think it's hilarious."

Sean didn't recognise the voice. It was eerily creepy and mildly irritating.

"What is hilarious? Who is this?"

"In time, Detective. First, I want to show you something. Are you near a laptop?"

"Sure."

"The art of murder, dot com. Hurry."

The line went dead.

The art of murder dot com? Seriously?

Out of sheer curiosity, he pulled his laptop out of his suitcase and shoved it on the table beside the phone, tapping his foot as he waited for it to load. He couldn't remember the last time he'd updated his technology. Sean had decided if it loaded up porn, it served its purpose.

After dozing slightly, he perked up as the computer finally loaded. He opened Internet Explorer. Clicking on the address bar, he typed in the address that had been dictated to him. www.theartofmurder.com. A blue bar spread across the address bar as the website loaded.

Once he'd seen the website, Sean rapidly roused to a state of full alertness and almost fell off his seat. His body went stiff, his jaw dropped and his eyes flung wide open.

Where had these pictures come from? Who had taken them? What did this guy want?

As if willing the phone to ring, he was reward by the shrill sound of the call tone resonating throughout the room again. Sean picked it up before the first ring had ended.

"C-c-cunt," was all Sean could stutter.

"I know, I know, I know."

"How did you get these?" Sean demanded.

On the screen before him was an image of himself, much younger, but still recognisable. Naked. In bed with another man. A penis in his hand. His lips on the other man's chest. A girl laughing at the camera as she took the photo.

"Tell me about this picture."

"Tell you about this picture?" Sean was ready to choke this guy.

"Yes. Or I will send the link out to everyone. Your colleagues, your ill, demented mother, your nagging ex… your daughter…"

He sucked in a sharp breath.

My daughter?

He willed himself to stay calm. Though he was livid, boiling up with anger, he had no choice.

"I am straight; you hear me? This was when I was twenty and a bunch of us had a thing with a bunch of girls."

"Looks like a bunch of guys to me."

"You fu-" Sean abruptly halted himself. He was on the edge of the bed, screwing up pieces of paper and leaflets from the bedside table in his spare hand, ready to smash the laptop against a wall. "We tried it once. Tell me you never explored your sexuality."

"How embarrassing."

"Who – the fuck – are you?"

The man paused. "I'm the man you're looking for."

Sean vigorously shook his head, willing himself to calm his breathing. The moonlight outside the window reflected on the overgrown blades of grass. He focussed on this for a moment. Distracting his mind. Telling himself to think clearly.

Eventually, his breathing settled. In. Out. In. Out.

"I'm listening."

"Good, Detective. Don't bother to try and trace this call. Don't try and trace the website. You will waste your time. Besides, those are against the rules."

"Rules? What rules?"

"I'm glad you asked, Detective. Number one, you do not tell anyone about these calls. Obviously."

"You want me to lie?"

Sean was sure he heard a grin in the man's voice.

"I don't think you'll find lying too hard. Number two, you will answer the phone every time that I call. Whatever the time of day."

"And what do I get in return, arse-hole?"

"I won't send that website out to everyone you know. Rule three, every now and then I will throw you a clue to help you solve my next murder, then give you until 4.00 p.m. Isn't this fun?"

"And how many victims will there be?"

The voice took its time replying to Sean's question, as if they were considering it deeply. "Let's start with an easy one. Your clue for Wednesday, Detective, is 'Gloucester Docks.' Remember, you tell anyone about this phone call, website will be sent out and deal will be off."

Sean was speechless.

"And remember, Detective. Before you think about telling anyone the truth – these pictures are just the start. I know your real secret."

You know my real secret?

The call ended. Sean couldn't move.

Chapter Eight

ALISON BURST around the corner out of the estate, leaving her family home behind.

This will show them, she thought. *Just wait until they wake up and find me gone.*

Despite only being eight years old, Alison was a headstrong, determined young lady. When she had an idea in her head she would always carry it through, with no one able to tell her otherwise. That's why, when she had decided the previous night to run away, she knew she would.

The sun was slowly starting to rise and the traffic on the road was sparse. Having never crossed a road by herself before, she took extra care in making sure no cars were coming. Clutching onto a couple of coins she had found on the kitchen table, she sat on the step to the corner shop, waiting for it to open.

She allowed her mind to wander to the previous night's argument. Her older sister, Sharleen, had gotten her own way – again. Just because she was fourteen and pretty, it was as if she could do all the things Alison wasn't allowed to do: invite boys over, wear makeup, swear.

It was so unfair.

Alison had been told by her parents she would not be allowed to go to the cinema on her own – after Sharleen had come back from going with her boyfriend! "We understand you want to go out on your own, but your sister is much older than you are," her father had calmly told her. "We just care a lot about you, that's all. We don't want you to get hurt."

She had been on her own for over ten minutes now and hadn't gotten hurt. It was so ridiculous. If Sharleen got hurt, how would she be able to take care of herself any better than Alison could? Her father clearly did not know what he was talking about.

She rubbed her arms as she began to shiver. It was early morning temperature and a cold breeze hung in the air. She regretted not thinking to bring a coat. Still, she couldn't go back now; even though she would like to see the look on her parents' faces when they went to wake her up and found she wasn't there.

Alison noticed a black van parked a few metres away from her. The windows were blacked and it emulated a stench alike to rotten eggs.

She covered her nose, creating a gas mask with her hands.

The door to the van opened and a man stepped out. Alison stifled a giggle at his appearance. His hair was slicked to the side with too much hair gel, he wore braces attached to light-brown corduroys, and his shirt was checked. Alison considered the amusing juxtaposition of his clothes; how his shirt looked like that of a five-year-old, whereas the trousers looked like they were stolen from an old people's home. She did like, however, that he wore a red bow tie. This made him seem quirky – like a funny substitute teacher, or an amateur magician.

But her giggle didn't last long.

This man was staring at her. He wasn't moving, wasn't blinking.

Just staring.

Still. Vacantly watching her.

"I was just wondering…" he began, with more inflections and changes in pitch than were necessary. "… Where your parents are?" he finished, after leaving a strange amount of silence in the middle of the sentence.

Alison couldn't decide what to tell him. She knew she shouldn't give personal information to strangers because of that workshop she'd had at school a few days ago. She did, however, want this man to go away and leave her alone, and felt he wouldn't do this unless she gave him answers.

"At home," she told him, instantly regretting imparting such information.

A smile spread across his face. His unnaturally large smile reminded her of the Grinch.

"Well that's no good, is it?" he exclaimed.

Alison shook her head.

"Let's see what we can do to take care of you."

SEAN GOT to work an hour before everyone else. He had not returned to sleep. Instead, he'd stayed up making plans to track down this bastard before anyone else could see what he was doing.

He hurriedly typed 'theartofmurder.com' into the address bar, scanning the bare office before pressing enter. He closed his eyes in disgust once more at the sight of the photos.

He copied and pasted the address into the appropriate software, managing to produce the host's IP address. He rushed out of the station, fist bumping the air and typing a number into his phone.

"Hey man, it's Sean," he began. "Listen, I'm going to send you an IP address. I need the home address sent to my GPS as soon as you can… Cheers man, I owe you."

By the time Sean had gotten into the car and switched the siren on, the directions were already sent to his GPS navigation. He drove as fast as he safely could.

SEAN TURNED off the siren as the GPS told him he was approaching the destination. He did not want the bastard (as Sean had decided to refer to him) to have any inclination that he was about to be caught.

As Sean entered the estate, he began to recognise it. A bush by the entrance, bigger than Sean had expected it to be, seemed familiar. As did the circular field in the middle of the road.

Hang on. Why do I know this…

He used to refer to this circle as 'the green.' The bush used to be his fort.

Surely not? This is too much of a coincidence.

As Sean pulled up outside the address he had been given, he felt numb. Unsure how to react, he shook his head at his own stupidity. He felt his nails dig into the palm of his hand as his fists clenched.

He got out of his car and entered the door to his childhood home.

Inside was a toy car on the floor, facing directly at him. Attached to it was a note that read:

. . .

I SAID this was against the rules.

SEAN THREW the car across the corridor, smashing it into bits against the wall.

Chapter Nine

"YOUR CLUE IS 'GLOUCESTER DOCKS.' You have until four."

Sean repeated the words over and over. Even if he couldn't stop this bastard's sabotage of his character, he could still stop any more death.

He considered what might happen if he came clean. What if he just bit the bullet and took the humiliation of the whole department seeing the photos?

But the photos weren't the problem.

It was the last words the bastard had said to him that plagued his mind:

"Remember, I know your real secret."

If this guy wasn't lying, then… it would be too much. He couldn't do it. However much his conscience told him to, he just couldn't.

What if he did come clean?

What if people did know? How would they react?

He'd known of a police officer who had kept secrets and ended up in the clink. After he'd been released, he'd never been the same. He barely even talked anymore; he'd completely retracted himself from everyone he knew.

I can't go to prison. I know how a police legend would be treated in prison.

Sean dialled Jack's number as he sped across town centre. For a moment, he thought about the irony of working for the police whilst speeding and talking on the phone.

"Jack, fetch yourself and two more plain-clothes cars and meet me at the docks."

"Why, Sean?"

"I'll tell you when we're there."

He hung up, mildly irritated by having to explain his reasoning; he shouldn't have to justify himself to Jack. Though, this did make it clear to Sean that questions were bound to be asked.

He was going to need an explanation for his tip off.

As he mulled over the possibilities, he remembered the message from yesterday's corpse; *Have you received my message Sean?* Could he somehow link that message to the docks? Sean knew the pieces were there, he'd figure it out somehow.

He pulled up at Gloucester Docks, exited the vehicle and evaluated the area. He couldn't cover the whole length of the docks by himself, he'd need support. There was no way he was going to be able to do this alone. Which was disappointing, as in solace was how Sean liked it. The only reason he kept Jack around was because he was a good lackey, who wouldn't get in the way of Sean's independence. Sean worked best without interference and he knew it.

A few minutes went by as Sean stood beside the water, his coat floating in the wind. The cold early morning breeze contrasted with the sun poking through the clouds, causing a conflict between the chilly draught and the warm rays. He took a sneaky swig of whiskey from the bottle in his coat pocket and considered the most prominent points of the docks for a murder to occur.

The most obvious cause of death would be drowning. Another alternative could be hanging from the bridge.

Jack pulled up beside Sean, followed by two cars containing detective constables in plain clothes. Once Jack had climbed out of the car, he paced toward Sean.

Sean checked his watch. 9.30 a.m. It was going to be a long day.

"Sorry I'm late, I was Skyping my daughter," Jack explained, straightening himself up. "What's the plan, Sean?"

"This is where today's death will take place, Jack."

Jack's eyebrows narrowed. "How do you know that?"

"Tip-off."

"What was the tip?"

Jack was already doing Sean's head in.

"It was the clue yesterday," Sean sighed. "The body. It said 'Have you received my message?' When I was a child, I would put messages in a bottle here and send them off, thinking they would go to sea. I don't know how the killer knows it. But this is where I believe the next murder will be."

It was a good lie. Made up on the spot, with enough detail that more questions wouldn't be asked. Sean's hunches were usually right, so his track record worked in his favour.

"Okay, boss, your call," Jack confirmed. "So what's the plan?"

"Stakeout," Sean stated, realising he had not yet had a coffee. "Each officer stationed along the canal, monitoring any suspicious activity. Radio contact on the half-hour."

"Roger," Jack nodded.

"Let's catch this fucker, Jack. Let's catch him so I can go home."

Jack turned to pass on instructions to the constables.

"Oh, and Jack-"

Jack swivelled back.

"Get us a coffee."

THE DAY DRAGGED ON, and 3.30 p.m. arrived. Sean couldn't have been more tense. His muscles were poised, adrenaline coursing through his veins. His thoughts mulled over all the things that could go wrong. He rubbed his eyes and attempted to shake himself awake, assessing the area, continuously darting his eyes back and forth. He was glad he could leave August to continue with the investigation in all the other areas; the less he had to dip his toe back into that pond, the better.

People walked by. Families, couples, workers, drunks. None of them even a little bit aware of the filth that rotted their home. None of them aware that they were walking on a potential murder site.

"Anything?" Sean spoke optimistically into his radio.

Jack and the other officers each replied. "Negative."

The bastard said 4.00 p.m.

Sean removed his coat. He flexed his legs. If he needed to run after someone he'd want to do it without his coat.

His eyes didn't move from the clock on the dashboard as 3.40 p.m. came. As did 3.50 p.m. As did 3.59 p.m.

Sean looked up and down the docks, readying himself to give chase.

4.00 p.m.

This is it. This is when he said it would be. I don't know what I'm looking for, but I need to be ready.

4.01pm.

He stood in the open. The killer would know he was there. There was no point hiding himself.

Sean surveyed the area once more, looking up and down the docks, peering in the boats, looking across to the old factory.

He rechecked with the others on the radio. Nothing.

People sat outside a café, drinking, catching up with old friends. People in suits hurriedly walked by, engrossed in busy conversations with their Bluetooth. Joggers went jogging. Couples kissed before staring lovingly in each other's eyes.

No sign of any killing.

Could the bastard have lied? Sean thought it for a moment. But he knew this profile of killer. They were honest. Killing may not be against their ethics, but lying was.

Eventually, 4.10p.m. came around. Sean's phone rang. Sean had been hoping it would be Jack, saying that he had the killer detained.

"Mallon," Sean answered.

"Sean, there's been another murder. We need you over here," came the frantic reply of August.

Sean grew confused. "Where?" There was nowhere along the canal that wasn't being monitored. The murder couldn't have gone unnoticed.

"At a pub in Gloucester," responded August. "The pub is called The Docks."

Chapter Ten

"YOU FUCKING IDIOT, YOU FUCKING IDIOT!" Sean told himself over and over.

He repeatedly punched the steering wheel as he swung the vehicle around the corner. He shook his head at his reflection in the rear-view mirror. His jaw ached from gritting his teeth.

How could I be so bloody stupid? Of course it was a trick. Of course, of course it was a fucking trick!

As Sean pulled up at The Docks, he urged himself to refocus. Needed his game face on.

It was another old British pub. When Sean arrived, police tape already surrounded it. August came out to greet him. Sean signed in, put on a protective white suit, and followed August along the dedicated path to join the Scenes of Crime Officers in the dining area of the pub.

There, he met the body of Alison Smith.

Eight-years-old.

Alison had been propped up against a seat, held in place with a nail in each bicep. In front of her was a plate of untouched food; what Sean assumed to be irony by the killer.

Her hair was perfectly brushed and her nails recently painted. Safety pins had been stuck through her cheeks to hold her mouth in a permanent smile. Sean struggled to tell if she was clothed, due to the amount of blood engulfing her.

On the forehead of the girl was the message:

HAHA.

THE ROOM WAS SILENT, officers of all ranks poised in motionless terror, gaping at the body.

Sean's stomach churned, a queasy sensation overwhelming him. This was new territory for most officers. They worked in Gloucester; their average day was dealing with sheep wandering off from a farm.

Not this. Not horrific, senseless killing.

He could feel their stares, watching him, looking to him to see how they should react.

But Sean couldn't give it to them. He wished he could be anywhere but there, adamant stares burning his skin.

The thought of having to endure a psychopath hunt again mortified him. He got out of it for a reason.

Sean remained rooted to the spot as officers carried out their work around him. Time moved at lightning speed, but Sean's heavy feet imbedded to the floor. He wanted to hurt himself in the worst possible way for such a glaring error. The girl had not only been killed, but humiliated. He stared at Allison Smith for what seemed an eternity.

The familiar sight of red filtered his vision.

Dread and guilt consumed his gut until it made him choke.

His hands, once more, held. The smell of Alison's body made him gag in the same way as Alexander Shirlov's had.

He fumbled out the room. The crime scene officers had finished and the Police Search Team were entering, looking for any sign of a nail gun or similar weapon that could have been left behind.

Sean had worked with this profile of killer before. This man would not leave the evidence they were hoping to find. Not unless he wanted them to find it.

As he leant against the wall of the pub, he swallowed three sertraline pills. He noticed August glancing at him. He saw the look in August's eyes reveal his hesitance to approach Sean. August could see the anxiety he was forcing Sean to go through.

Sean grabbed one of the crime scene officers by the arm as they exited the crime scene.

"Tell me..." Sean began, mustering the energy to ask the question he was about to ask. "What was the time of death?"

"Er," came the uncertain reply, taken aback at having their arm restrained. "We can't tell right now. The landlord came to open the pub and the body was stiff, been propped there about an hour ago. We reckon sometime before four."

Sean faintly nodded as the man released himself from Sean's grip.

August finally grew the courage to arrive at Sean's side. "The Family Liaison Officer has gone to the parents to give them the news."

"Get Jack to do the profile and witness statements. Let's gather at the station and go over what we've got."

"First we need to-"

"August, please. Just give me a minute."

AFTER SPLASHING a sink full of water over his face and begging his reflection to be strong, Sean returned to the

Murder Incident Room and stood with August and Jack. On the board in front of them were seven pictures, each of a different body. All of them were arranged in a precarious pose.

Sean thoughtfully stroked his chin as he took in the images of the various bodies, the other officers gathered behind him in suspense.

"Got anything?" August prompted, in an attempt to interrupt the awkward silence of the room.

"Where's that detective constable from yesterday, Elizabeth something?"

"Here," she announced, stepping forward.

"What did crime scene officers say about location of death? Did they all die at the location they found them?"

"Apart from Shelley Dalel, no. They appeared to have been transported."

"See, you couldn't do this. The body would be too stiff to move following their death, he must have-"

Sean interrupted himself with a thought. The thought grew into an idea. The idea grew into a plan.

"Jack, you've seen the post mortem reports. What is consistent? What sticks out in all of them?"

"They have been moved, like you said."

Sean shook his head. He turned his back to the pictures and addressed the room. It was at this point he realised why they needed his help.

"Each of these bodies has been drained of blood. Why would he do that?"

Shrugs of shoulders and blank faces met his gaze.

"So he could drink it?" Elizabeth offered, a perplexed expression accompanying an idea that caused Sean to roll his eyes.

"He's a psychopath, Officer, not a vampire," Sean dismissed her, causing a few chuckles. "We need to stop trying to track the killer and start tracking the bodies. The blood was drained out of all the bodies. This is the constant feature throughout all of them, apart from Shelley Dalel – who was left at the death scene with all her blood intact."

"Post mortem lividity…" August mused.

"Exactly! He needs to drain the blood from the bodies to avoid them becoming too rigid, so he can move them. Blood is thick. It stinks. It's not like water. He needs some way of disposing of it."

"So we look for reports from people with blocked drains?"

"No, he won't report it himself, that would get him caught. We need to look for a report from a neighbour, complaining about blocked drains with a really bad stench."

August clicked his fingers and pointed at Sean, shaking his head in astonished disbelief. "You heard the man, get going."

The room came to life. All officers were in front of computers or on the phone to plumbing companies, tracking down any possible complaints over the last six months. Within half an hour, they had come up with three possible locations.

Sean dismissed the first one, as the stench had been explained by the discovery of dead rats and animal faeces. The second was of a house that wasn't occupied, which Sean cross-examined with complaints of homeless dwellers, therefore giving an explanation as to why there was a high amount of wastage not being removed.

The third was a middle-class family estate. A number of neighbours had complained. Multiple warnings had been sent, to no response.

"This is it," Sean exclaimed. "Let's go."

He ran to the car outside, ordering Jack to stay and supervise as August attempted to keep up. Before they knew it, they were forcing cars to part like the Red Sea via their sirens. It was twenty minutes away, but they could make it in five.

Sean recalled what it was like to drive with the sirens on. It was one thing he missed; driving without flashing lights took so much longer.

As they turned into the estate, Sean's phone rang.

It was Jack.

"What?" Sean barked. Why was he interrupting an important sting like this?

"Sean, stop. Don't go in there."

"What? Why?" Sean grew irritable. He aimed a frown at August, who mouthed, "What?" back at him. Not only was Jack trying to give him orders, he was instructing him not to follow their strongest lead.

"Trust me, Sean, you don't want to go there," Jack assured him, pleading with him, urging him hopefully.

"Go to hell, Jack." Sean hung up the phone.

As August pulled up to the house, Sean's seatbelt was already off and his door already open. They approached the house with agility, automatically coordinating their positions, with Sean ahead and August dropping off. They frequently used to work together on operations like this and it didn't take long for them to get back to old ways.

Sean banged his fist on the door, "Police, open the door!"

No response.

"Police! Open up, now!"

They heard the unlocking of the door from inside the house.

Sean turned back to August. They nodded at each other. This was it.

Readying himself for whatever he found behind the door, he stared daggers at the handle, waiting for it to turn.

As the door opened, Sean didn't wait for a response. He

pounced instantly, taking the suspect down to the floor, mounting them with feigned aggression.

He froze.

He looked around. There were pictures of him and his brother on the walls. There were pictures of his parents' wedding day.

"What are you doing?" came the muffled cry from underneath him.

He looked upon the person he had taken to the floor. He looked upon the face of his mother.

"Mum?"

"Your mum did this?" August responded with clear bemusement.

Sean stood up and let his mother go.

"No. My mother has dementia. She barely even knows who I am. She'd just moved into a home with help, I hadn't been there yet…"

He leant against the wall, banging his head against it. He lamented audibly with exasperation. He let his guard down and put his arm around his Mother.

"Hi, Mum, it's me. It's Sean."

"Sean?"

"Yes, your son."

His mother pulled her head away in confusion. "My son?"

"Yes."

"Oh."

She looked to the ground, clearly working her mind hard to remember him.

"I'm here to make sure you're okay. Come on."

He led her to the living room and sat her down. He covered her with a blanket.

"Where's my granddaughter? I have a granddaughter?"

She sat up like a meerkat, showing the first bit of energy since Sean had arrived.

Sean looked to the ground with a sigh. He closed his eyes and took a moment.

"Let me just get you a cup of tea, Mum."

He put the kettle on and leant on the side. He shook his head to himself.

She doesn't remember me, but remembers a girl she hasn't seen for six years. Why…?

Sean finished making the cup of tea and took it to his mother. Once he'd made sure she was settled, he joined August in walking back to the car.

"I don't understand." August scratched his head.

"Isn't it obvious?" Sean responded as he took the passenger seat.

August shook his head.

"It's the same reason he wrote my name on all the bodies. It's the same reason he's—" He stopped himself as he remembered August didn't know about the phone call.

"What?"

"He's taunting me for fun."

Chapter Eleven

SEAN GLARED at the ceiling for most of the night. He hadn't arrived back at the hotel until 1.00 a.m.; he couldn't let himself. The killer was targeting him and he couldn't understand why. He mulled over the pieces of the puzzle in his mind.

The killer was clever.

The killer had used the areas he knew had poor CCTV coverage and a pub where the owner had conveniently overslept that day.

The killer had not only anticipated their clues, but had used them against Sean.

Jack had even suggested the The Dock's owner could be a suspect, but Sean dismissed it, citing the reason as a lack of motive; when it was in fact because Sean did not recognise the man's voice as the one on the phone.

He thought about his daughter. He pictured her face. He thought about what he'd do if anything like this ever happened to her.

Feeling slightly drunk from the contents of multiple beer

cans now lying empty on the floor, he picked up his mobile and dialled in a number.

"Hello?" the woman's groggy voice answered, evidently having just been woken.

Sean realised he had not thought about what he was going to say.

"Hi... Hi, it's Sean."

"Oh my God, fuck off Sean."

"I just want to see my daughter. I got the letter from your attorney, but it's not fair. I just want to see my daughter."

"Go to hell, Sean. Don't ring back again."

The line went dead.

He growled at the phone and threw it at the bedside table. He slumped onto his back, seething at the ceiling, contemplating the pieces of his life that were left scattered.

His daughter had been taken off of him due to his post-traumatic stress disorder. His wife couldn't even stand to be around him anymore.

His job had become too overwhelming since he couldn't stand the sight of blood anymore. He'd grown incompetent.

And now. This investigation he'd been dragged into. He'd already messed it up by engaging the nutcase on the phone.

He reached for his medication.

Dear sertraline, at least you'll never leave me...

3.00 a.m. came and Sean still lay wide awake, jumping from negative thought to negative thought. Never had he been so tired yet so awake. He could even smell his foul stench, but just couldn't be arsed to wash.

Finally, Sean began to doze. But, just as he fell into the lightest of slumbers, the shrill ring of the phone jerked him awake. He rushed out of bed and almost dived on it.

"Yes?"

"You failed, Sean."

"Fuck you, arse-hole, fuck you. I didn't fail, you fucked me."

"Actually, Sean, you were not the one I fucked."

The horrible bastard on the end of the line cackled at his ill-tasting joke.

"At least now, my friend," the voice continued, "you know that you cannot track the IP address nor the blood remains to me. You must understand that you are, fundamentally, useless."

Sean shook his head to himself. What was he doing?

"What do you want?"

"Have a look on the website."

Sean hastily opened his laptop, bashing in his daughter's name as the password. The website was still open from the previous night. He hit refresh.

Below the demeaning pictures was a front page headline with a picture of Sean leaving a suspect's house, staring at his blood-soaked hands.

Sean knew what this was. Sean knew what the killer was getting at.

"Very clever. Very, very, clever," Sean sarcastically declared.

"I know, I know. It's just a taster from your sad scrapbook of heroics. Now, what about what's in your safe?"

Sean stuck the phone between his ear and his shoulder as he withdrew the safe from his suitcase and frantically opened it.

His jaw dropped and his legs quivered.

It was empty.

"You've been in my room?" he growled, doing all he could to cover his terror with anger.

"Tell me about the evidence in your safe. I'm holding it in my hands right now."

"I'm not telling you shit."

The killer grew hostile. "Tell me or I'll send it to everyone you know! What would Detective Superintendent Daniels say about this?"

Sean respired with exasperation.

"It's evidence on a case I was on."

"What case?"

"I tracked down a sex offender who was making child pornography. I killed him in self-defence."

"In self-defence? What really happened, Sean?"

Sean closed his eyes and took in a deep breath.

"You know what happened."

"Oh, I want to hear it from you. Tell me about what I'm holding in my hands."

Sean bit his bottom lip, agitatedly fiddling the duvet between his fingers. He looked around his room, as if he was going to find an escape hidden in a corner somewhere.

"It was part of the report from the Scenes of Crime Officers. I hid it."

"And what does it say?"

"It says, the gun in the dead sex offender's hand, it wasn't at the right angle for where the bullet holes in the wall are. It implies he didn't actually have the gun in his hand when I reacted in self-defence."

Even though no one was around to see him, he still covered his eyes as he felt them fill with tears. He scrunched up his face, holding in his despair. He would not give this guy what he was after.

The voice sounded smug about the silence, knowing he had truly gained the upper hand. "Well, well, well. And you said I was an arse hole."

Sean's clenched fist thudded the bedside table, sending his alarm clock and whiskey bottle flight. His breathing quickened, his heart raced.

Calm down, Sean. Calm down.

He couldn't let this guy affect him. He needed to keep this guy happy. He needed to keep him happy so he could catch him.

"I should have told people about you. I should have done it today. I should have taken the embarrassment and used every available resource to track you down, you complete and utter fucking cunt."

Sean couldn't help it. He hadn't felt this close to being out of control in a long time.

"But you withheld the information. Just like you did before. And now another girl has died."

"*Fuck you!*" He screamed into the phone, straining his voice so much it started to crack. "What the fuck do you want from me?"

"This is the tip of the iceberg, Detective. How's your daughter?"

Sean ran his hands through his hair and rested his forehead on the table. His legs shook with fury, his arms trembled with terror. His insides twisted, tearing into painful pieces. Adrenaline pumped through his body with nowhere for it to be directed to.

"Good," the killer spoke, confirming his pleasure at Sean's torment. "Now. Your clue. As ever, you have until 4.00 p.m. Would you like the clue Sean?"

He took a moment to compose himself.

"Yes. Yes, I would like the clue."

"I use this to see," replied the killer. Then, he hung up.

Sean threw the phone across the room, bellowing in anger so hard his lungs burnt.

Chapter Twelve

SEAN DROVE INTO THE STATION – this time, with less pace. | It was 7.00 a.m., and he knew he had until 4.00 p.m. to stop the murder. Driving under the speed limit helped his mind-set, ensured he remained calm. He needed to think clearly if he wasn't going to fall for the bastard's tricks again.

"I use this to see." "I use this to see."

However many times Sean mulled over the words, they just became more and more ominous. The way the clue had beaten him the previous day still felt sore.

Despite hating to admit it, he knew the bastard was clever. Sean knew the killer simply wished to give Sean the impression that he *could* be caught.

Seeing as the killer knew every sad and pathetic part of Sean's life, he entertained the idea that the clue may be personal to him. After all, most of what the killer had done was to taunt him.

Sitting outside the station, he pulled out a notepad and listed all the places he thought the clue could link to.

Eyes are used to see, that is obvious. But what else? An

optician that sold glasses? Laser eye clinics? He added them to the list.

What about seeing in the figurative sense? Something that helps you to metaphorically open your eyes? Somewhere that educates you? Universities, maybe; a library, or a museum.

What if he wasn't referring to the word *see*, but instead the letter *C*? 'I use this to help me *C*. Places that helped you learn the alphabet? Schools, maybe?

Sean knew he was clutching at straws.

Sean surveyed his list. He did not have the resources available to cover all locations, which meant he would need to be selective. He discarded the more elusive ideas, ones that had too many dots to connect, and was left with the following:

1/ Opticians

2/ Laser eye clinics

3/ University

He could do this. He could have a policeman stationed at each point. At least this gave him a shot.

He called Jack. "Jack, don't ask questions, just do this for me, and do it quick. Station constables on a stakeout at the following places." He read out his list. Even though Jack was clearly agitated for not being able to enquire why, he obediently agreed.

This could leave Sean time to do the real police work. He took the scrapbook directly to Elizabeth.

"I'm worried someone may have been in my room," he told her. "Can you run the prints on this?"

She nodded and took it away to the laboratory, leaving Sean standing at the front desk, drumming his fingers against the surface. His eyes wandered around the room. A woman with bright-red lipstick and fishnet tights sat handcuffed to a chair.

"So, what are you in for?" Sean asked her, sniggering as he turned away. She scowled at him.

Elizabeth returned ten minutes later, handing the scrapbook back to Sean in a plastic sealed bag.

"It's got your prints on it," she told him.

"And…?"

She shrugged her shoulders. He gazed at the scrapbook in his hands, shaking his head in disbelief.

How could he be so much better than us? This doesn't make sense.

As he stood in that morning's briefing, the Scenes of Crime Officers revealed that they had some more information.

"We have DNA that links each body to each of the places the killer has used to taunt you," Janet Gresham, the lead in this unit, told Sean. He remembered having a crush on her back when they worked closely together on his serial killer case a few years ago. She had long, blond hair and prominent bosoms. It took all he had to concentrate on what she was saying and not the inappropriate cleavage hanging out from underneath her white lab coat. "It is clearly the same DNA, which makes it clear that we have a suspect."

"Have we identified the DNA?" Sean interrupted, urging her to get to the point.

"It took us a fair bit of digging," Janet assured him. "But we have a match. And an address. Name is Ben Diggle."

Sean smiled genuinely for the first time in days.

"Excellent, let's go."

SEAN SPED through the town centre, sirens on, flashing blue lights. Cars rushed to the side of the road in front of him to let him through. Jack clutched the passenger seat next to him. Sean didn't care. One thing he had definitely missed was the thrill of driving this fast; his adrenaline was pumping at the thought of catching this bastard.

Within a minute, they had driven the five miles across a busy town centre to the address they had been given. It was in a council estate, where many of the houses were burnt out and people hung out on the street. These people stopped and glared at the sight of a police car. It was not a place he had previously been welcomed.

Sean couldn't care less if he was welcomed. He was so close.

Sean was already at the door of the house by the time Jack had managed to fully lurch himself out of the car. Sean booted the front door until it broke down and he burst in.

"Police, get on the ground!" he screamed.

He ran through the vacant living room and kitchen. When he got to the dining room, he came across a bemused man sat at a table with a spoonful of cereal poised halfway to his mouth.

Sean didn't give the man a chance to respond. He dove on him and took him to the floor, forcing him on his front. He handcuffed him as he read out his rights.

A crowd had gathered as Sean dragged Ben Diggle to the police car and shoved him in the back. They shouted at Sean, calling him 'pig' and 'filth.' Sean wasn't bothered. He'd heard it all before. Nothing was going to ruin this moment for him.

Still, a thought niggled in the back of his mind; it was too easy.

Chapter Thirteen

SEAN AND JACK stood in the adjacent room to the interrogation room, staring through the one-way window at their suspect. Ben Diggle was sat still, handcuffed to the table. August Daniels was beside him, setting up the recording equipment with another officer.

Ben's legs were quaking and his eyes darted around the room. He wore a grey suit, clearly ready for what would have been a day at work. His hair was slicked back with too much gel and he was slightly overweight. They had found little in his house in the way of possessions or memories; he was divorced, and a bit pathetic by the look of him. They had found nothing incriminating and they had looked hard.

Sean studied him with folded arms. If it was an act, it was a damn good act.

"How long we got?" Sean requested as August entered the room.

"I've extended it to thirty-six hours," August answered. "We've got until then to get something credible to the Crown Prosecution Service and charge him. We have around half an hour until his lawyer gets here."

"Okay. Let's make a start."

August gave the nod to the officer standing next to him. Sean knew him well. His name was Graham Shooter, an officer old enough to be approaching retirement, but still the best lead interviewer Sean had known. Graham showed no signs of fatigue in his age, still as calm and calculated as he had always been.

Sean had been incredibly grateful for Graham when catching the serial killer a few years ago. Graham had managed to get the suspect to talk himself into so many circles before they delivered their intelligence, thus proving the man was a liar; as far as Sean was concerned, if Graham couldn't do it, no one could.

Sean watched avidly as Graham took his seat opposite Ben. He smiled gently, introducing himself on first name basis to make sure he made the conversation feel personal.

"I'm just going to ask you a few questions, Mr Diggle," Graham spoke so softly you'd have thought he was a librarian rather than a police officer. "If you could answer the best you can."

Ben nodded with frenzy. He looked like a deer caught in the headlights. Sean wasn't sure what to make of this.

"Can you tell me where you were at these times?"

Graham passed a sheet of times across to Ben. Ben studied them closely before looking back up at Graham like a wounded child.

"I don't know, I… At home, I think."

"Can you be sure?"

"I spend all my time at home. I can't think of any reason I wouldn't be."

"Do you live alone?"

Ben nodded.

"So you have no alibi for being at home alone?"

Ben shook his head.

"You understand how that looks to me, right?"

"I don't even know what I'm here for. I don't know how it looks…" He looked like he was about to well up and cry.

Graham sighed.

"Let's start with the first time on the sheet. Can you recall your actions on this date?"

"Yes, I, er… I went to work–"

"Where do you work?"

"In a tyre company."

Graham nodded, stretching out his hand as a signal to continue.

"I left there at around 4.30, 4.35 maybe. I went to the Co-op on the way home to get myself a pizza. I stayed at home and watched TV."

"What did you watch?"

"I don't remember."

"Try."

Ben lifted his head back and closed his eyes, visibly urging himself to think.

"Jeremy Kyle, I think. Then maybe some football."

"Who was playing?"

"Arsenal versus Spurs."

"Oh really? You a gunners' fan?"

"No, I just like a good match."

Graham nodded, watching Ben with a keen interest.

"Who won?"

"Arsenal, I think. Two to one."

"Oh yeah, who scored?"

"I don't remember."

Graham leant back in his chair, producing another sheet of paper from his folder. A picture of the first victim. Ben flinched and turned his head away, coughing in repulsion.

"Have you ever seen this person?"

Ben clenched his eyes shut to avoid having to look at the corpse and shook his head.

"Okay," Graham stood. "I'm just going to leave this with you for now."

Graham left the room and returned to Sean and August.

"Well?" August looked to him.

"I don't know. He doesn't fit the profile. He seems to be safe in his whereabouts he's accounted for. I don't know how I can talk him around this one. I don't think it's him."

"It's got to be," Sean enforced, louder than he intended.

Sean glared at Ben Diggle, narrowing his eyes, firing daggers with his stare.

The DNA was right. Surely.

Sean's temperament fell as his rabid eagerness to catch this kill overtook him.

"I'm going in," Sean announced, taking his coffee and joining the suspect before anyone could object.

He entered the interrogation room smugly, placing his coffee down and sitting back in his chair, his legs spread out. He studied Ben Diggle for a few moments. Smirked at Ben. Even winked at Ben, Sean figuring he'd be extra arrogant. Why not?

"Mr Ben Diggle," Sean began. "Father of two. Divorced once. Works at a local tyre company. Pays taxes, stays out of trouble on a rough estate and is a generally polite man. Or so everyone thought."

Sean leant toward him.

"Tell me, Ben. What's it feel like to be caught?"

"For what?" pleaded Ben, terror in his voice. He was trembling. "I have no idea what I am here for." Tears appeared in the corner of his eyes. "Please, I am no one."

"I use this to see," Sean whispered, knowing he was playing a dangerous game with the others listening in. "What does that mean?"

"I don't know, I don't know riddles. Please, I don't know what I'm doing here."

Sean slammed his fist down on the table, causing the table to shake and Ben to jump. A tear was now rolling down Ben's cheek.

"I always found crying on cue impressive. You've put on a good act. Let's start with the first body I saw. Shelley Dalel."

Sean threw an open file on the table in front of Ben, revealing a picture of Shelley's dead body. Ben gagged and recoiled. It occurred to Sean how Ben's accent was different to that of the voice on the phone.

"Oh my God…" Ben wept.

"Shelley Dalel is her name."

"I know who she is," Ben spoke up. "She is my ex-wife."

Sean was silenced. Something sparked in his mind.

"Your kid?"

"Is in foster care," Ben pleaded.

"What's her name?"

"Felicia Howard."

Sean froze. The second victim.

"Do you have any links to a girl called Alison Smith?" Sean enquired.

"Yes…" Ben claimed, almost in a whisper. "She's my niece."

Sean buried his head in his hands. It was at this point he knew he had been set up.

Chapter Fourteen

HE AND HIS girlfriend loved milkshakes. As they stood patiently in line, he switched his decision between chocolate and banana again and again. In front of them were a family of two parents and a young girl ordering milkshakes as a special treat. He remembered how his mother started his love of milkshakes with a similar routine.

He imagined the young girl face down across his living room floor. Naked. Dead. Sodomised.

"Are you going to have chocolate sprinkles?" asked his girlfriend.

"Oh yes, that would be lovely," he replied.

By now Sean Mallon and the police would have been interrogating Ben Diggle for hours. He still had a while before 4.00 p.m., which is why he decided lunch with his girlfriend would be nice.

He would still have time. Needn't be sloppy.

Taking a second to admire his girlfriend, he smiled. She was a primary school teacher, with glasses the size of her face, long brown hair and a long, flowing skirt that fitted with her hippy fashion. Her voice sounded like honey. She truly was sweet and beautiful.

But that young girl.

Hung up by her feet.

Defecating blood. Begging for her life.

"What would you like, sir?"

"I would like banana please. With chocolate sprinkles."

The young girl dropped her milkshake and immediately burst into tears. He crouched down beside her and picked it up.

"Here you go," he smiled at her, scooping up the slight spillage of ice cream from the floor and returning it to her hands. "Now don't you go spilling your milkshake. That's the worst thing that could ever happen to you."

Her tears halted. She stared at him. Motionless.

"What do you say?" her mother prompted.

"Thank you," she cautiously said to him, her wary stare hovering.

"No problem." Her blood. All over his bare torso. Her face smashed to pieces. "You go run along now."

As he stood up, his girlfriend congratulated him on being such a good guy. He nodded and slurped his milkshake.

SEAN RETREATED to the other side of the mirror, where the rest of his team were observing Ben Diggle cowering in his handcuffs.

"It's not him," Sean declared.

"How the hell do you know that?" August objected, refusing to let their strongest lead slip through their fingers.

"It's just not," Sean weakly justified. "Graham's right, he doesn't fit the profile. His link to all of them. It's too easy. He's been set up."

"I am not about to let him go, Sean!"

"Well I'm not about to charge him. It isn't an act. He's nobody. His link to all the victims is good, yes – but it's a taunt. This killer somehow, I don't know…"

Sean found it difficult to explain intuition to someone who relies solely on complete justification. Besides the fact that Sean had interactions with this killer, his intuition had helped him solve some of the biggest murders the department had come across. It was what made him so good at his job. Which was something August never seemed to understand.

"Is there anything else we can get out of him?" enquired Jack, eager to help.

Sean considered this for a few moments. His trail of thought led him to think Diggle could still be an asset. Sometimes, Jack was more use than Sean would let himself admit.

Sean returned to the interrogation room with paper and a pen, which he presented to Ben. Ben looked up at him like a puppy.

"I want you to write down every other person that could link you, Shelley Dalel, Felicia Howard, and Alison Smith," Sean commanded. "Leave no omission, the slightest, obscure link is fine. Write down what the link is. Once I am satisfied you have given us enough detail, you will be free to go."

SEAN AND JACK made their way through the list, using police records and the Internet to consider each person Ben Diggle had named. He hadn't liked letting Diggle go, but he knew there wasn't much more you could get out of a coward like that.

Sean instructed the investigation team that each person on the list was both a suspect and a potential victim. Sean had managed to stretch their resources even further than the various officers he had stationed around town following up on the 'I use this to see' clue; he now even had officers operating surveillance on each person Ben Diggle had written down.

If the killing was going to happen at 4.00 p.m., and one of them was either perpetrating a murder or facing death, the case would be solved today.

This has got to be it.

The list that Ben Diggle had given them showed five names. They were as so:

1/ Jenny Staff. Felicia's foster parent. She had come under intense abuse from Shelley when Shelley was denied her children back. She had allowed Alison to visit her cousin.

2/ Harbid Ahmed. The paediatrician to both Alison and Felicia.

3/ Caron Rose. School teacher of both Alison and Felicia.

4/ John Glee. Shelley's ex-boyfriend. He had a paternity test done on him and Felicia as he claimed she belonged to him, but it turned out negative. He had faced some hostility from Alison's parents as a result.

5/ Bill Haman. Ben's best friend and godfather to Alison.

Sean surveyed the list, knowing he would have to put it aside soon. The time was 3.50p.m.

He was waiting, poised, on edge. Anticipating the call to one of the victims houses, to find that the killer had been detained. He had a feeling about it. He had a feeling this could be it.

Once 4.10 p.m. had passed, apprehension and self-doubt had replaced his feeling of optimism. No one had called yet. No attacks had been made. No police intervention from any of the officers stationed around town. He had even radioed each police surveillance team to double check their suspects. No unusual activity.

Within a minute, Sean had the phone call. Another body had been found.

The body of Ben Diggle.

Chapter Fifteen

STANDING INSIDE THE PUB, Sean ran his hand through his hair in disbelief once more. It was called The Eyes and Spectacles. 'I use this to see' had been the clue. He had been duped. Again. What a fool.

Ben Diggle's body was laid upon the floor with lacerations to the neck, showing clear evidence of asphyxiation.

The following was written upon the body:

DO BETTER, Sean.

SEAN CLASPED his arms around his chest, lifting one hand to cover his face. He couldn't look. It was another clear taunt, aimed at getting to him.

And it was working.

The familiar sight of red entered his peripheral vision. He considered how much he hated not being able to feel any kind of anxiety without panicking.His breathing quickened.

His heart thumped.

Why me? Why is he after me?

He popped a few more pills and left the Scenes of Crime Officers to do their job.

"I think we've got a pub killer," August announced to him.

"No," Sean dismissed.

August moved his face closer to Sean. Feeling August's breath on his face, Sean grimaced, but without moving; he was adamant he would stand his ground.

"You're here on an advisory basis, Sean, don't-"

"Exactly, I can leave any time. You need me more than I need you. So if you want my expert opinion, take my expert opinion. It is not a pub killer; it is a public killer. It's voyeurism he's after, not fucking beer."

August walked away like a dominant gorilla. Sean scoffed. He thought about his private investigator office. The bottle of whiskey in his drawer. His rich clients would never ask him to look at dead bodies; they would only send him after fornicating ones.

He took Jack back to the Murder Investigation Room. Once in the car, he got on the phone to the detective sergeant and instructed him to organise his detective constables in bringing in the people from Diggle's list.

Sean and Jack worked late into the night, questioning each and every person on Ben Diggle's list in scrutinising detail. Midnight passed and they were sat alone in the Murder Incident Room, surrounded by empty coffee cups and open files.

"Nothing," Sean stated. "Fuck all. Absolute shit that we can work with."

Jack remained silent. He didn't think that agreeing would help his mentor's rage. The clock approached 2.00 a.m. and they had both been working themselves ragged.

"Let's go to bed, meet back here in the morning," Sean announced. "There's nothing we can do now."

Jack nodded and they dispersed. He had no intention of going to bed.

SEAN STILL SAT by the phone at 4.00 a.m., waiting for the call. Wrapping himself in a blanket he used to let his daughter use, he took in its loving scent. It still smelt of mud and Play-Doh and he found that comforting.

It was at this point he realised just how tired he was. His eyes were sore. Like they were bursting out of their sockets. He had been awake for over thirty hours and his body was starting to suffer.

He browsed theartofmurder.com on his laptop. Nothing had been uploaded yet. His mind wandered and he found himself on his ex-wife's Facebook profile. He looked over photos she had uploaded the previous night. She was in a nightclub, with her girlfriends, dancing, taking lip-pouting selfies and smiling.

He looked further back in her photos in hope of finding pictures of them together, on one of their holidays or a day out. His heart fell as he found no such photos. All those memories they had shared were removed.

He minimised the Internet page and opened one of his folders. Inside were pictures of his daughter in many scenarios; smiling at him, hugging him, going on a walk with him, building sand castles. A feeling of warmth grew over him, the tingling of love trickling down his body. He was so proud of her, wherever she was.

The phone shrieked, interrupting his trail of thought.

"You're late," Sean grunted. Tiredness was slowing down

his mind. He wished he'd come up with something far wittier.

"To suggest that I am late would be to suggest that we have prearranged a time. I phone when I want to, Sean. You are at my liberty, not the other way around."

"Those are big words," Sean observed, still attempting to get one over on him. "I assume you are university educated?"

"Looking for a clue Detective?"

"How about we meet," Sean smirked. "I could give you a clue or two."

"Very big of you. No, we do not meet yet."

"At least give me a name then."

"You can call me…" he left a moment of thought hanging in the air, allowing Sean to quickly grab a pen and paper. "Victor."

Sean jotted the name down.

"Victor," he repeated. "Victor what?"

"Not yet, Sean," Victor chuckled. It was okay, he had a name. Whether it was his real name or not, the name told Sean plenty about him. Sean noted down in brackets on the pad, '(psychologist)', thinking he could acquire an expert's opinion on the choice of name. Then it occurred to him that he'd have to explain how he had this information and maybe that wasn't a good idea.

"Well, Victor. What dirt have you put on the net about me today?"

"Why don't you have a look?"

Sean clicked on the tab he already had open and hit refresh. As he had expected, the contents of his safe were now published on the Internet. A picture of the body holding a gun at the wrong angle. A picture that proved the gun was never there in the first place.

"One of your proudest moments?" asked Victor.

"You arse-hole. This doesn't prove anything," Sean

declared, shaking his head. He would do anything he could not to have to relive this moment as his mind had been doing every day for the past year.

"Doesn't prove anything?" Victor almost choked himself on his laughter. "This was the first photo of this guy after Scene of Crime Officers entered the scene! You *stole* it! Doesn't prove anything? Doesn't need to! It's enough to send you to jail as it is."

"He was a sex offender. I killed him in self-defence. The public don't care about any of the fine lines. They hailed me as a hero without even knowing the full story."

"No, Sean, they will care. The faith the press put in you, all the talking to the therapist you hated, all those psychological evaluations, the whole reason the legend that is Sean Mallon fell off his perch. All a lie."

"The world is better off believing that lie!" Sean cried out as he stood, consumed by frustration. "So what else do you have on me? You got pictures of me sucking any more dicks, covering up any more pricks who deserved to die, huh? Huh? What do you want from me!?" He screamed so loud he was sure he must have woken the next few rooms over.

He sat back on the bed, panting, rubbing his spare hand over his face. He was sweating, growing even more incensed by the distant chuckling he could hear on the other end of the line.

Clambering his hand forward, he grabbed a bottle of whiskey off the floor, bypassed the glass and poured it straight into his mouth. He took a few large gulps, neglecting the need for air, rejecting the sharp initial sting of the alcohol.

Once he had dropped the bottle, he sat still, staring to the ground. It was at this point he realised no one had spoken for at least thirty seconds.

"What do you want from me?" Sean emphasised each syllable in his calmest, huskiest, aggressive whisper.

Victor remained silent.

"I'm an alcoholic too, but I bet you knew that. You've been in my room. You took my stuff; you know, the whole place stinks of it. That is why I live alone. Because no one can deal with it. That enough? Should I stop there?"

After a few moments of silence, Sean managed to calm his breathing down. His leg was still shaking. His fist was still clenched.

He closed his eyes. Counted to ten. Breathed.

Four slow, sarcastic claps came from the other end of the phone.

"Well done, Sean, well done. But, as I said, I haven't even gotten started yet."

Sean closed his eyes and bowed his head.

"The sex offender came at you with bare hands and you came at him with a kitchen knife. Your use of self-defence was unlawful, so you lied."

Sean clambered for his pills, washing them down with a large swig of whiskey. His eyes felt dry. He could feel his pupils throbbing in time with his pulse. He urged himself to keep it together. He told himself to be a man.

"Hate the truth?"

"Fuck. You."

Victor gave a long, audible, satisfied, "Mmmm."

"That's all for tonight. Sweet dreams, sunshine."

Victor's end of the line went dead.

Sean wept into his hands, holding back tears, too tough to cry.

He sent the whiskey bottle hurling toward the wall, smashing it into pieces.

Chapter Sixteen

6.30 A.M. SEAN arrived at the station. He spent the two hours before everyone else arrived searching the police system for murder suspects called 'Victor. Nothing recognisable or consistent with the profile of death occurred. Not that he expected it to. He expected it to be a fake name; but if Victor wished to torment him, he wouldn't have been surprised if there was another taunt waiting for him somewhere as a result of this name.

Having found nothing, he went out for some fresh air and to raid the shelves of the local pharmacist for caffeine tablets. He had been awake for days and was pretty sure he wasn't going to be finding time to rest in the imminent future.

As soon as he stepped back through the station doors he addressed Elizabeth, who was sat at the front desk.

"Find me every person on file that may not be on the immediate system called Victor," he commanded without taking a breath, "Male, between eighteen and forty, printed off."

She nodded. "Sure, Detective."

"And do not tell anyone else about this," he demanded, shooting Elizabeth a deadly look, hoping she obeyed.

Sitting in the waiting room with a coffee in his hand, he stared gormlessly at his feet. After twenty minutes of daydreams spinning between worries of Victor and memories of his daughter, he was interrupted by Elizabeth with the reports he'd asked for.

He spent three hours sifting through the files, taking in every page, reading every line, studying every photo. He grunted at officers who tried to talk to him, even waving away Jack who arrived requesting instructions, barking at him to, "Just follow up some leads."

Nothing. Not a person whose murders or crimes followed a pattern even close to that of the killer. He looked to the clock and let out a big huff upon seeing that it was already nearly midday. He took a sip from his now cold cup of coffee and threw the files into the bin basket.

This meant that either Victor was a fake name, or the bastard (as Sean had previously referred to him) had no criminal record. He'd known from the start it was an elusive search.

He sat back and rotated around in his chair. It may be childish, but spinning had always helped him think. All the other officers were out on errands; interviewing various witnesses, suspects, following up vague leads; anything he could do to force them out of the office and avoid those awkward questions about what he was doing.

Despite knowing his morning's search would be all for nothing, he still found it hard to contain his fury at the despondent, meaningless hunt.

Sean screwed the coffee cup up and threw it onto the carpet next to a dry coffee stain. He burst to his feet and marched through the station, kicking the kitchen door open.

His thoughts went to his daughter and his ex-wife as stared gormlessly at the boiling kettle, willing himself to focus and think rationally.

A coffee cup that read Best Husband Ever still sat in the cupboard in front of him. The cup that used to be his when he worked there. In a spurt of rage, he picked the cup up and launched it across the room, smashing it into pieces.

He was so stuck on his thoughts of love lost, he ended up over-pouring the kettle into his plain cup, thus burning his hand with the excess water. He swore to himself and ran his hand under the cold tap.

Refocus, Sean, you bloody idiot. Refocus!

As Sean left the kitchen, Jack burst through the door, spilling more of his coffee. Before Sean's grumble could turn into audible swearing, Jack's excited mood overwhelmed him. Like a child in a candy shop showing their parents a new sweet, he seemed desperate to tell Sean his news.

"Boss, we got a lead!" Jack announced, punching his fist into his hand, elated.

"Who?" Sean sceptically barked.

"Jenny Staff." Jack raised his head and his eyebrows slightly, a huge smile spreading from cheek to cheek. "One of the people on Diggle's list that we interviewed last night."

Sean dabbed a paper towel over the coffee on his trousers. "What's the lead?"

"She called this morning. Said she's remembered a guy hanging around Felicia Howard's school when she picked her up."

"Why didn't she say this yesterday?"

"She said she'd only just thought about him and it occurred to her to ring. Sean, he matches the description."

Sean fist bumped the air.

"Where is she?" Sean requested, far more energetic and alert.

"We brought her in, we have her next door in a holding room."

Jack led the way as Sean hurriedly followed him into the adjacent room.

Jenny Staff sat on the edge of the seat, her hands fiddling nervously. Her glasses were small, but big enough to cover her freckles. Her auburn hair was long, over half a dozen necklaces around her neck. Her skirt was multi-coloured, like a rainbow, and her voice fit her appearance.

"Hi, Ms Staff." Sean stuck out his hand and shook hers. He noted how much of a soft, weak handshake she had. Sean was mildly irritated by timid people, as it meant he would have to change his approach to being all understanding and sympathetic.

"Good morning," she replied, her voice soft and quiet.

Sean sat down beside her, careful not to invade her space. "My name is Sean Mallon. I am the lead on this case. My partner tells me you have something you think could help us?"

"Yes. A man was hanging around the school… It didn't occur to me until… Or I would have sooner…."

Sean put a hand on her shoulder. "It's okay. You've come to us at a great time. If we get a sketch artist in here, can you give him a more detailed description?"

"Of course."

Sean smacked his hands together with excitement. Jack ushered in the sketch artist and within minutes they had a clear picture of the suspect.

"How old do you reckon?" Sean mused to Jenny.

"Late 30s, early 40s. He was… off."

"Jack, get this picture and match it with all CCTV footage from each crime scene. Follow any man that looks remotely similar. Get the detective constables on it now, I want that within ten minutes, go."

Jack nodded. He stood for a second to make sure he had heard all the instructions Sean had hastily barked at him, before hurrying out of the room.

"Ms Staff, you have no idea how helpful this will be. Thank you."

"I'm glad I could help," she delicately replied.

"Is there anything else you could tell us about this man? Any distinguishing features? Any particular movements?"

"He…" Jenny contemplated her words carefully. "He… was a little socially weird."

Sean nodded and took his notebook out.

"I mean, I know you can't just *look* socially weird…."

"It's okay, put it however you would like to put it. I'm not going to judge the words you use. Just anything that helps us get a profile of this guy."

"Well…" She paused, looking up at the corner of the room to think, then returning her eyes to Sean. "He was just… odd. He walked weirdly, he looked at things in a bizarre way. Just… socially weird, I guess. Yeah. I don't really know how else to explain it."

Sean scribbled her words down.

"Did he have any abnormal twitches? Any mannerisms you could describe?"

"He mumbled to himself. He walked with, like, all his joints moving."

Sean nodded. Bizarrely enough, he actually knew what she meant.

"What was he doing?"

"He was just standing there, wandering around. He was there briefly. Didn't stay long. Didn't really stay still."

Sean nodded. "Thank you, Miss Staff, you've been so helpful." He finished writing down in his pad. "I'm going to leave you in the capable hands of another officer to take down some more information. Thank you again."

The Art of Murder

He sorted out another officer to take down the more mundane information and left them alone. He entered the Murder Investigation Room and it was buzzing. Sean couldn't help but be slightly impressed with how Jack had organised everyone. There was a station prepared for each of the murders, with a few officers gathered around each screen, producing CCTV screenshots of a man who looked identical to the sketch artist's drawing. Within half an hour, the walls were covered, a separate display for each murder; all with images of their suspect. There was a man of similar height, build, and description around the location of each murder. No definite footage of abductions or violence, but a presence at each scene at least.

"Do we have a name yet?" Sean asked.

"No," Jack replied, looking around at the other officers working, who in turn shook their head.

"What?" Sean's eyebrows narrowed and his voice grew agitated. "How do we not have a name?"

"We've run all the footage through each database we have, he's not in there," Jack responded without hesitation. "We're trying, but we don't know."

"Right, someone take the photos to the witnesses on Ben Diggle's list and see if they can identify him. Then take him to any witnesses at any of the other murders."

No one moved.

"Now!" Sean bellowed.

Jack promptly clicked at a few officers and led them out of the room.

Sean slumped back in his seat and surveyed the images on the wall. He studied this man, learning more about him with each picture. His fashion was always similar; bow ties, checked shirts, braces, which meant he had quite a niche, distinctive fashion sense. His eyes were wide, like he stared a lot and rarely blinked. This dress sense and odd appearance would surely make him clearly identifiable to witnesses.

Surely, they would have a name soon?

As the room emptied, with every detective constable allocated a different task, Sean was left alone with his thoughts. Without even realising it, he had closed his eyes. They felt good to be shut and finally resting. His eyes and his body felt weary and he knew he was running on empty.

He tried to think nice thoughts. He imagined being back with his daughter again. He thought about how close they were to catching the killer. Thoughts about how he was finally of use.

As he entered a deeper sleep, his thoughts changed.

A man appeared. On his knees. The same man he had seen in his mind every day for the past year. Charging toward him.

His knife sinking into the man's throat.

Blood trickling through Sean;s fingers.

Sean screamed.

His lungs hurt, but still he screamed, louder and louder, harder and harder. He screamed at himself to stop screaming, but he didn't.

The blood thickened.

Hands became heavier.

Until, without even knowing how, his whole body was drenched.

He could smell it. The decay of the body. The blood trickling down his face. He could even taste it.

He jolted upright and opened his eyes. August stood above him with his hand on Sean's shoulder.

"Whoa, Sean, you were screaming."

Sean looked around, attempting to gauge where he was. It was dark again.

"Sorry, I think I must have…" Sean quickly adjusted his

mind, realising he was back in the Murder Investigation Room. "How did the enquiry go?"

"We've got a name. Victor Crane. Identified by two of the others off the list."

"Address?"

"We don't know. A last known residence, yes, but–"

"Fantastic, let's go get him."

As Sean jumped up, August put his hand on his shoulder and kept him from becoming too eager.

"Listen, Sean, maybe you shouldn't."

"What?" Sean realised he was squaring up to August. He relaxed his shoulders and backed down.

"You've been great help to us in solving the case. Now we need to track him down. We don't know how long that's going to take. I think you need some rest."

"I'm not leaving this case."

August sighed.

"I'm not asking you to. I'm just saying, there's nothing you can do *right* now. Until we've apprehended him, it's just a waiting game. Once we've found him… We'll call you if there's a change. Just go home."

For once, August spoke sense. Sean knew he had been brought in for identifying the killer's identity, not for the apprehension. Now it was time to try and track the killer; which could take days, months, even years.

He would leave Jack with them. If today had proven anything, it was that Jack could be relied upon when Sean needed him. He felt okay with this decision. Without responding to August or acknowledging the correctness of his suggestion, Sean called a taxi and headed back to the hotel.

The whole way back, the images of the blood grew greater and greater, painted in the forefront of his mind

As soon as he returned to his hotel room, he grabbed a

near-empty bottle of whiskey and clambered into bed. He closed his eyes, and for the first time in over three days, he slept freely. He slept deeply. So deeply, in fact, that when 2.00 a.m. came, the phone ringing didn't wake him up at first.

Chapter Seventeen

THE PHONE'S ringing lasted longer than it had before.

Eventually, Sean stirred. His eyes opened and his vision slowly came into focus. Rubbing his eyes, he sluggishly sat up. He knew without having to be fully aware that the ringing was summoning him to his next phone call with Victor. He considered, for a moment, what would happen if he didn't answer.

The police had Victor Crane's identity now. They were tracking him. The taunting could stop.

Sean's involvement could stop.

He could go home. Back to taking pictures of scumbag rich people fucking other scumbag rich people. He'd had enough of lying to August; harbouring secret phone calls with a killer was more than he had ever intended to do.

Then this thought was overcome with the sight of the corpses. Victor's threats. The victims. He decided he needed to humour Victor Crane, even if only to keep the line of communication going.

Sean answered the phone and spoke without thinking. "Arse-hole."

Victor chuckled back at him on the other end. "I know, I know."

"People are dying; this isn't a game."

"Then what is it?"

"Juvenile genocide."

Sean could hear a fist slam on a table in appreciation as Victor guffawed with laughter, barely able to breathe.

"You're a psychopath."

"I'm a visionary!" Victor declared without missing a beat. "And my will be done."

Sean sighed. "Well, come on then. What dirt have you dug out on me today? What's on the website? Do I even need to look?"

"Nothing."

Sean frowned. "Nothing?"

A few moments passed, then Victor spoke cautiously and clearly.

"I think we should meet."

Sean deliberated this for a few moments; this could be the defining moment of the case. This could be his opportunity.

"Sure," he spoke, attempting to sound casual. "Shall I meet you at your house?"

"Well no, considering that address has been raided today."

This guy is always one step ahead.

"Okay then, Victor, where?"

"The train station. Half an hour."

Chapter Eighteen

SEAN KNEW it wasn't wise to enter a suspect's house alone. But, honestly, he didn't care.

The intelligence was that this man had made multiple child pornography films in his basement. The intelligence also suggested he was doing the same, right now, with more innocent children.

Yes, he'd called it in. Yes, he knew he should wait. Uniformed officers would be there soon, ready for a raid, possibly even firearms. But how could he wait? How could he hang on, knowing that there could be children in that house getting filmed and raped at that very moment?

Alexander Shirlov. Thirty-nine. Single. A butcher. A brother. A son.

A paedophile. A rapist. A killer.

Enough. Sean ran against the door, taking three barges to knock it down. He ran through each room, finding nothing.

It wasn't until he stood completely still that he heard the sounds.

Noises of pain coming from below him.

Crying. Pleading. Screaming.

Charging forward, grinding his teeth, he kicked down the basement door and called out, "Alexander Shirlov! Come out!"

He took a few steps back. He allowed the figure of a man to emerge out of the room. Glasses, an overweight belly, greasy hair and poorly shaved beard. The man's disgusting appearance only enraged Sean further.

"You are under arrest. You do not have to say anything–"

Before Sean could finish, Alexander Shirlov charged toward him, rugby tackling him to the floor. Sean landed a few punches into Shirlov's back as they wrestled on the ground. Shirlov engulfed his arms around Sean's legs and he pushed him with all his force, trying to break free. It was no good; this man had a lot of weight and he had put it all onto Sean.

As Sean was pinned down, he looked to the basement entrance. Proceeding from the room he had heard all the painful screams coming from, were three unclothed boys, fleeing, with tears streaming down their cheeks, whimpering with terror. Sean's jaw dropped as he saw them.

They were all crying. They were all young.

"Get out! Get out of the house!"

They burst out the front door, screaming for help, shielding their eyes from daylight they hadn't seen in a long time. Shirlov jumped to go after them. Sean pulled him down. Shirlov raised his fist toward Sean.

Sean didn't even think about what he did next. He saw the kitchen knife resting on the dining table. He took it.

He lunged it into the throat of his enemy.

Shirlov fell to the floor, clutching onto the open wound, desperately trying to stop the bleeding.

Sean collapsed to his knees, gawking at the blood on his hands. It oozed slowly through his fingers and onto the floor. His eyes went from his hands to Shirlov.

Shirlov's body faded. It was lifeless. Eyes stopped moving. His chest stopped expanding with breath.

"No, no, no, no," Sean whispered to himself.

He wasn't supposed to be entering the house alone. He was supposed to wait for back-up.

This would cost him. His career. Possibly even his freedom. His opponent was unarmed. He went in without permission.

A court would see this as excessive force.

He darted around the house, looking in each room. Eventually, he psyched himself up enough to enter the basement. As he entered, he skidded to a stop. Body odour and damp filled his nostrils. Thoughts of acts he knew had taken place there made him gag.

A broken mattress. Two video cameras. Chains. Whips. Everything you imagine a torture den would have.

And a gun. A gun that sat upon a table. That gun would do.

Sean wiped some sick from his mouth. Covering his hand with his sleeve, he picked up the gun, transporting it up the stairs and into the hand of Alexander. He took two shots at the wall across from the corpse.

He noticed the flashing of lights through the window. He had momentarily gone deaf to the noise; so much so he hadn't heard the sirens approach, nor the gathering of a crowd outside.

As he walked out the door, he was greeted with cheers, camera flashes and cries of, "Hero."

He stood in that moment forever. Staring at his hands still dripping with blood.

I killed a man. I killed a man. I killed a man.

His thoughts focussed on four solitary words. Even though he was too stunned to react, he knew his decision would cost him far more than just his career.

Chapter Nineteen

SEAN LEANT against the wall of the station platform, beholding the clear night sky. A few drops of rain landed on his forehead, but it didn't bother him. He had always liked the rain. It was probably the only thing he and his ex-wife had in common.

He glanced at his phone: 2.32 a.m. Despite the time, he was wide awake. Ready for whatever was about to come. He had made a quick decision before he left to hide a GPS tracker in his back pocket and link it to his laptop in the hotel room. If there was a need for him to phone someone and make them aware of what was happening, they could easily find him through the screen of his laptop. He was prepared for anything.

As he watched 2.32 a.m. turn to 2.33 a.m., his mobile rang. It was an unknown number. He slowly manoeuvred the receiver to his face and answered.

"You're late," Sean spoke.

"Head outside the station to the taxi rank. Do it now."

Of course, it wasn't going to be simple. Sean had to have no idea where he was going for the killer to feel comfortable.

He decided it was fine; he had his mobile and he had his GPS. He would need to put his faith in his ability to handle the situation.

He was ready. No need to be apprehensive.

He stepped out of the station, into the car park. There was one taxi; apart from that, it was deserted. It was a small station, not the kind he would expect many people to be boarding a night train. There were still many shadows, many places for people to hide, to be watching.

"Get into the taxi and pass him the phone."

"Why don't you tell me where I'm going first?"

"Do it now, Detective, or I end this call and we both go home."

With a slight hesitation, Sean walked over to the nearest taxi and got into the back.

"Evening," Sean began, not sure how to approach the taxi driver about having to speak to a psychopath on his mobile.

Sean pointed the phone toward him. The taxi driver posed a questioning look at him.

"Just take it. He'll tell you where I'm going."

Reluctantly, the taxi driver took the phone, saying, "Hello?" into the receiver. He gave a few grunts, acknowledging a few instructions. In a sudden moment, his face turned to horror. Without saying a word, the taxi driver handed the phone back to Sean, started the engine and pulled away.

Sean returned the phone to his ear, but the line had gone dead. Tucking it in his pocket, he looked out the window. The familiar view of shops he grew up with as a child passed him. He recognised one of the fields where his ex-wife used to watch him play football in his early 20s. He had taken his daughter there to visit the park

He didn't have time for that now.

After around fifteen minutes, the taxi driver pulled up on a bridge.

"We here?" Sean looked around.

"No," the taxi man replied. "The guy said to throw your phone and the GPS you've hidden in your back pocket over the bridge and get back in the cab."

"He wants me to throw my mobile and GPS in the water?" Sean replied with astonishment, fully aware this would depart him from his tracking system and only way of contacting someone should something go wrong.

"Please," the driver begged, "just do it. That way, no one gets hurt."

Sean contemplated for a moment what this man had been threatened with. What leverage did Victor Crane have on him? Realising there may be more resting on it than a wet SIM card, he obeyed. After noticing he had three missed calls from Jack, he rolled down the window, lobbed the phone and GPS out with his best overarm throw and wound the window back up.

Looking at the taxi driver's eyes in the rear-view mirror, he identified a tinge of fear. The man nodded and resumed driving.

Ten minutes later, the taxi driver came to a halt. Without a word, Sean got out of the cab. In the instant the door was shut, the taxi sped off into the distance, breaking the speed limit; presumably to check on his family's safety.

Sean found himself looking upon the entrance to a park. Leaving the road behind him, he stepped through the gate. The park was bare, disguised by trees and based around a river. In front of the river was a bench. On it sat a man, throwing bread to the ducks.

Sean remained stationary, contemplating how to proceed. He couldn't go in charging; jumping onto this guy and beating him to death wouldn't work, however much he'd like to. So, instead, he walked toward the bench and sat beside Victor Crane.

"Good evening, Sean. Or should I say, good morning?"

Victor turned and smiled at Sean.

Sean took a few moments to take in Victor's appearance, scanning for anything that would help to identify him. Victor's face was plain, except for a pimple at the bottom of his cheek. His hair was parted and flattened to his head, with copious amounts of hair gel holding each strand in place like glue. He wore a big anorak over a checked shirt, his top button done up, perfectly tucked in, with braces holding his sickly-brown trousers up. He guessed late 30s, early 40s.

He finally understood what Jenny Staff meant about 'socially off.' There was no other way to explain his mannerisms or his appearance. His presence was comforting yet unstable. His smile was pleasant yet chilling. His eyes glazed over sweetly, yet they sent the biggest chill down Sean's spine he had ever had.

"Good morning, Victor," Sean replied.

Victor threw the last remains of his transparent food bag to the ducks. The clueless animals gobbled up the bread, fighting each other over it. Once they realised feeding time was over, they returned to the river, leaving Sean alone with the killer.

"So what do we do now, Victor? Where do we start?"

Victor let out a large "hah" that came from his belly.

"Always straight to the point. You don't think that I could have brought you out for the company? Idle chit-chat? Life can get lonely. But you already know that, don't you?"

His voice was the pitch of a man but the tone of a child. Everything about it was off. Each hand rested on a knee with his legs parted, in perfect symmetry. He seemed like he could turn psychotically erratic at any moment, yet had the calmest demeanour Sean could recall.

"How about we start with how many people you've killed. How many would that be now?" Sean stuck his bottom lip out and raised his eyebrows.

"Oh no, no, no, no, no, no, no," Victor muttered to himself. "Let's instead start with those I have yet to kill. Now there is the conundrum."

"You're not killing any more people, Victor," Sean decided, making sure to use names so as to personalise the encounter; using every police negotiation tactic he knew. "It stops right now. When I arrest you."

"Rather bold, don't you think, Detective?" The way he stretched out the word 'Detective' made Sean's insides churn. "You think I'd invite you here for you to arrest me?"

"How about we stop measuring dicks and you tell me what it is you want. You tell me what it is you want from me, exactly why it is you are punishing me, and we go from there."

Victor chuckled to himself. A chuckle that lasted longer than was comfortable. "I like you, Detective. Why would I want to punish you? You're so much fun to play with."

Sean sighed and looked around the park. Empty. Trees blocking the view from surrounding houses. Whatever happened on this bench would be done in isolation. The only people who would know would be Sean and Victor.

Maybe he could kill him? The idea toyed with Sean's thoughts. He could. He could strangle him, or drown him, then claim he had a tip-off about the killer. No one would find the website. No one would prove otherwise.

He had done it before.

"So you called me out here for a chit-chat then?" Sean looked at him, deciding how he would do it, if he was to make his move. He had to remain cool. Avoid giving Victor any suspicion of what he was thinking.

"No, you're right. I didn't call you out for that. I called

you out because a young girl's life is going to be dependent on what you do next. I have her in captivity, and if you don't make the right decision, she'll die."

Sean froze. Any notion of killing him faded from his mind in an instant. Sean knew Victor could be bluffing; but knew him well enough by now to know that he most likely wasn't.

"Okay, you have my attention."

"The game is as follows – I have a girl in my captivity. I have three possible locations for you to choose from; each at a location thirty minutes away in separate directions. You following me so far?"

Sean stared back at Victor, refusing to dignify the question with a nod.

"Good," Victor took Sean's hostile silence as confirmation. "The girl in my captivity is hooked up to some kind of device; the specifics don't really matter. What needs to be made clear, is that the device will kill her in thirty-two minutes. Meaning you have a one in three chance of finding her."

"I'm not playing your sick game, Victor."

"But there is a twist! I will not tell you which location the girl is at. You must guess. And if you get it wrong…" Victor traced his finger across his neck to visualise a slit.

Sean stared back at him. If he called in the three locations, he could have uniformed officers at each location within ten minutes. Maybe it was time to come clean.

As if reading his thoughts, Victor smiled at him. "Don't even think about calling it in."

"Why not?"

Victor produced a photo of a red-headed girl, around twelve, with large glasses. The girl in the image was gagged. Sean felt a familiarity with this girl. He thought deeply. He tried to recollect numerous girls he had come in contact with. Where did he know her from?

"Keep thinking…" Victor smirked.

It struck him. Sean finally realised. It was the girl from the picture inside Jack's notepad. It was Jack's daughter. His partner's daughter.

Sean's eyes widened.

Victor produced a phone, telling Sean, "You can check if you like."

Sean snatched the phone and dialled Jack's number as fast as his fingers would let him. He shoved the receiver against his ear so hard he hurt his cheek. After three rings, Jack picked up.

"Jack, it's Sean –"

"Sean, thank God. My daughter, Lily, she's missing. My daughter has gone missing!"

Sean dropped the phone to the floor. His mouth dropped open. He sat agape. He looked to Victor, whose smile only incensed the rage in Sean's gut.

"I know, right?" he spoke.

As Victor leaned over to take the phone back, Sean grabbed him by the collar and threw him to the ground. Mounting him, he laid his fist into Victor's face repeatedly until his knuckles grew sore. After Victor's nose began to bleed, he lifted his fist back in the air and looked upon the bastard. Victor laughed. He was enjoying this far more than Sean was.

"Where is she, you fucker? Where is she?" Sean commanded.

Victor continued laughing.

Sean decided to try a different tact. He grabbed hold of Victor's neck and dragged him to the river. Grabbing hold of Victor's hair, he lifted his head back and dunked it into the water. He held it there until the bubbles stopped. Then he held it there a little longer.

Sean pulled Victor's head out and faced it.

Victor was still laughing. The bastard was still laughing.

Sean was enraged.

"Where is she?"

"You're not going to find out if I'm not alive to tell you!" Victor practically sang his declaration.

Sean let go of Victor and stood over him.

"I'm calling this in," Sean asserted, reaching out to snatch the phone off Victor. "You can go to hell."

"If you call it in, she'll die. Jack's daughter will die."

Victor continued to laugh as he looked up at Sean, coughing up water in between each guffaw.

Sean sighed, clenching his fists. There was no way to beat it out of this guy. Sean had to play his game. For now. He hated it, but it was true. It was the only way.

"What are the three locations?" Sean spat through gritted teeth.

"Worcester Quarry, Pitville School and Gloucester Docks. You can choose which one you're going to as we make our way to my car."

Chapter Twenty

LILY SLUMPED in her seat with her arms folded and a slouched posture, epitomising the image of a petulant child. She could hear her mum talking to her head of year in the office behind her. She could hear it all too well.

"She's struggling to fit in with other children in her year."

"How?"

"When any child tries to approach her, she just withdraws herself."

"Well what's wrong with that?"

"Nothing. It's just some of the girls tried to take her book off her… she became violent."

"How violent?"

Lily covered her ears. She was fed up of hearing it. It was enough that she had to put up with the stuck-up girls in this school. She wanted to be left alone.

She wanted her dad back. She hated it when he was away.

Her mother left the head's office and looked to Lily with a solemn stare. It was a caring, disappointed stare that only

The Art of Murder

mothers could give. She smiled a fake smile, leading Lily back to the car.

It took seconds before Lily was in tears. With a cry of, "Oh, Lily," her mother's arms were instantly around her, holding her tightly. She squeezed Lily close, kissing her on the head repeatedly.

Sitting back, she gave Lily a pack of tissues.

"Can we just go home?" Lily sobbed.

Her mother nodded and obliged, driving away in uncomfortable silence. After a few nervous glances at her mother, Lily finally broke the tension.

"What did they say?" she asked, already knowing the answer.

"They said you got into a fight with a few girls who tried to steal your book."

"Well, they tried to steal my book."

"You're twelve, Lily, you need friends. They were trying to be friends."

"Funny way of showing it."

BAM!

Dusty smoke engulfed the car, accompanying the slam of the airbag in their faces. The mother and daughter gripped their seats as the car swung around and around like it was never going to stop. Lily could hear herself scream, yet couldn't feel any sound coming out. She looked desperately to her mother as she clasped the side of her seat.

"Mom?"

It was no good.

Her mother's eyes were closed and blood trickled down the centre of her face. As the dreadful sight mixed with nausea from the accelerated spinning, Lily threw her lunch up over the gear stick.

The motion of the car slowed as it slammed into the side

of a wall. It was sent another 180 degrees by another car flying into the boot.

Lily cried. What else could she do? Her mother wasn't responding, the air bag was practically suffocating her, and she couldn't understand what was happening.

A minute passed. Deadly silence screamed into the car. There was a deafening ringing in her ears and she could feel her mouth fill with blood.

She could hear no shrieks, no onlookers, nobody coming to see if she was okay.

Just her and the sound of her breathing.

Smoke drifted into the car. Fumbling at her seatbelt, Lily eventually unfastened it and clambered out of the door, landing hard on the gravel of the road. She looked at the palms of her hands, cut by the bumpy cement.

Footsteps approached. She couldn't figure out from which direction, or how close; senses were completely disorientated.

A shadow grew over her. The figure of a man stood tall. She struggled to see his face as the sun behind his head created a silhouette.

"Are you okay?" he asked. Although the sentence was caring, his voice sounded deep and sadistic.

"My mum, she's hurt…"

The man crouched down beside her, revealing a tweed shirt beneath a bow tie and a cheeky, sinister grin.

"It's okay, you're going to come with me."

"What? Who are you…"

"Victor. My name's Victor."

Chapter Twenty-One

SEAN HANDCUFFED Victor's hands behind his back, opened the door to his Mini and threw him onto the backseat.

Sean assumed the driver's seat, looking for the keys, which he found already placed in the ignition. Victor's distant cackling filled the car. Sean knew Victor had let him handcuff him. Sean knew Victor hadn't put up a fight because he would still be one step ahead of him.

Sean didn't care.

Lily was the priority.

Sean made an instinctive decision.

The quarry.

Victor spoke that word the strongest, or so Sean decided; he knew he was clutching at straws, but he had to decide, as otherwise the one in three chance would go to zero chance. What's more, he knew the fastest route there, so he was fairly certain he would arrive there in thirty minutes.

Victor was still laughing.

"Shut the fuck up!" Sean growled.

Sean slammed his foot on the accelerator and screeched

away. He cut every corner and almost tripled the thirty mph limit. It didn't matter./ He would not let his partner's child die, and he would not let Victor Crane win.

Victor sat himself up and his laughter faded into an infuriating smirk. Sean could feel Victor's eyes on him in the rear-view mirror. Not even blinking. Watching Sean's every move.

I'm not going to get there in time. It doesn't matter how quickly I drive, I can't make it.

"If she dies, I'm going to kill you," Sean announced. "Maybe not right now, maybe not even today. But I will choke the life out of you and watch you die. You wait, you scrawny little bastard."

Victor's smirk grew even bigger. This incensed Sean. He punched the steering wheel. He was struggling to think straight.

"You don't get it, Sean, you don't get it," muttered Victor. "Right now, you're giving me everything I want. This is all going according to plan. You may kill me, you may not. Either way, it will only happen if that is what I wish."

"I *will* kill you."

"Detective –"

"Cut the Detective bullshit, my name is Sean Mallon. And yours is Victor Crane. We may as well use them."

"As you wish – Sean." As soon as Victor placed an irritating emphasis on his name, Sean regretted his outburst. "So you know, if you think at any point that you are winning this game, remember this."

Victor looked him dead in the eye and pronounced each word slowly and particularly. "I know whether you are going to the correct location."

His mad cackling resumed so extravagantly that he struggled to stay sat up.

Jack looks up to me. He relies on me. Now I'm probably about to let his child die.

He checked his speedometer. The car was going fast. He didn't care. He had seen the locket Jack wore around his neck, the picture inside his notepad; Sean knew what Lily meant to her father.

Fifteen minutes.

The look on the face of Alexander Shirlov.

The horror. The mouth open. The struggling to breathe.

Flashbacks raced around his mind like manic rats batting against a cage. The image played havoc with his ability to think objectively.

Could I bring myself to do it again? To kill Victor if I had to? After it's destroyed me?

His mind was scattered. He checked his pocket for medication, his hand traipsing over an empty bottle.

Shit. I can't do this without medication.

His blood raced through his veins, heart beating against his chest so hard it caused him pain. He willed to slow it down, to keep him level-headed. It was useless.

Without his medication, he was useless.

Ten minutes.

His breath caught in his throat, making him choke. He coughed on his own oxygen. A glance in the rear-view mirror. Victor watching him with an oversized grin.

"Prick."

Five minutes.

What if she isn't at the quarry? What if I have to deliver the news to Jack that his daughter died and I could have stopped it?

What about when I have to admit that I'd been in contact with the bastard who killed his daughter this whole time?

He ran his spare hand down his face, slapping himself in attempt to focus. He needed to be objective. He needed to focus on the task at hand.

Three minutes.

He overtook a slowly moving car, narrowly missed a pensioner crossing the road, and spun around the corner. The quarry wasn't far now. But three minutes was unlikely.

Shit. What if I don't make it?

He regretted taking Victor to the floor and punching him. Not because it didn't feel really, really good; but because it wasted time. He hated playing this sicko's game. This guy was truly in control.

"You're not going to make it..." Victor sang from the backseat, grinning from ear to ear, only just loud enough for Sean to make it out over the ringing in his ears.

I'm not going to make it. I'm not going to make it.

Two minutes.

He told himself it wasn't over yet. The quarry wasn't far. He was close. But was he two minutes close?

He broke suddenly as he came to a corner he saw late and swung around it, leaving skid marks behind him. Victor smashed his face onto the seat in front of him. For a fleeting moment, Sean enjoyed unleashing pain on Victor.

A glance at the clock refocussed him.

Location reached.

He broke hard, applied the handbrake, and rapidly launched himself out. He left Victor behind. Victor didn't want to escape. Victor wanted to stay and witness this.

It was the middle of nowhere.

Sean fumbled through the darkness, reaching for his next step. He had the lights of the car behind him pointing at the quarry, but he saw nothing.

He slowed down. Looked around. High and low for any sign of any girl.

Then he saw it.

A young girl's body down the steep drop of the quarry, upon the floor in the middle of the crumbling rocks. Four torches were strapped to poles pointing towards the corpse. Covered in shadows, Sean made out an axe, attached to some strange device he assumed was a timer. The axe was stuck in a log the body was tightly tied to with rope. The body had no head.

The head was a few yards away.

Sean fell to his knees, grabbing crumbling bits of the ground in his hands and letting them fall through his fingers. He cried out as tears left his eyes.

He had seen many dead bodies. He had never, however, seen the open-mouthed expression of a young girl's face on a head that lay away from its body.

He couldn't move.

The contents of his stomach made their way to Sean's mouth and he threw them up over the side of the quarry.

The girl was brown-haired. It wasn't Jack's daughter.

Victor had killed another innocent girl just to toy with him.

Sean's head fell to the ground. He checked his body once more for medication.

His breath wheezed.

Jack's daughter spun around his mind, the face from the photo implanted on his cranium.

Then he was in Alexander Shirlov's house.

Running out of the basement. What those children endured...

What Lily would be enduring...

Sean's legs gave way as he collapsed to the floor.

His breath punched his ribs. His chest boomed, legs vibrated, arms shook.

The severed head. Shirlov's body.

He clasped his sweaty hands together then out again.

Focus on the breathing. Focus on the breathing.

He fumbled for his medication once more. Even though

he knew they weren't there, he hoped that somehow his pills had turned up.

They hadn't.

Sean turned and looked toward the car.

He forced himself to his feet, his legs wobbling, his breath struggling.

Victor sat in the back, watching him, showing no movement.

Sean took one step toward the car. Then another. Slowly, he placed each foot down on the gravel and calmly returned himself to the Mini. Opening the driver's door, he climbed in and sat down.

He looked at Victor smirking at him in the rear-view mirror.

"That's not my partner's daughter."

Victor shook his head in the way a parent would to a young child who had gotten a question wrong.

"I assume she is elsewhere."

Victor raised his eyebrows, pursed his mouth together and nodded, the way you would with a child who had identified how they had misbehaved.

"I assume she is dead."

He smirked. He kept his head still.

"Give me an answer, Victor."

Victor sighed a big sigh. He looked out the window to admire his work.

"No, she's not dead. She wasn't at any of the locations. That was some other girl I found this afternoon. I'm just fucking with you."

Sean's fists clenched so tightly his nails dug into his palm.

"You still have her, though. Don't you?"

"Yes. Yes, I do."

Sean looked up at the sky, scrunching up his fists. He had to keep his aggression in. He had to keep calm. He could not beat this guy if he gave him the emotional response he was after. Victor wanted to be pummelled. He wanted Sean to lose his cool.

"And what is your plan now? Are you going to keep her? Do I have to go through some other sick game to get her?"

"No, Sean. First you need to give me the keys to my handcuffs."

"I'm not doing that."

"If you don't, her throat will be cut."

Enough.

Sean kicked open the car door, flung open Victor's door and grabbed him by the throat. He dragged the psychopath to the ground.

"What you going to do?" Victor laughed at Sean with a playful snarl.

Sean grabbed Victor by the neck and lifted him against a large rock he found at the side of the quarry. His teeth gritted like metal cogs, his face scrunched aggressively and his hand squeezed around Victor's throat so hard he thought he may snap it.

In that moment, he didn't care.

"Where is she?"

Victor remained quiet. He choked for air, gasping desperately, all the time still grinning.

"Where is she?!"

"Kill me… And you'll never know…"

Sean grabbed a large piece of stone with a sharp point, pricking the tip of his finger to test it and drawing blood.

He knelt upon Victor's chest, grabbing a fistful of hair to pull his head back and present his neck. He pushed the sharp end of the stone against his throat. He put pressure on it, making sure Victor could feel death coming close.

"I'm going to count to three."

"Good for you!"

"One…"

Victor stuck his tongue out and blew a raspberry at Sean.

Sean applied more pressure.

"Two…"

"Murderer."

Sean froze.

"You going to do to me what you did to Alexander Shirlov? You going to plant a gun on me too?"

Sean's aggression dropped. He rooted to the spot.

Hands, covered in blood once more, only this time around Victor's throat.

Just like Alexander Shirlov.

He threw the stone away, dropping heavily onto his back.

I almost did it again… What's wrong with me…

Victor rose to his feet. "Get in the car," he demanded.

Sean complied.

Chapter Twenty-Two

VICTOR DROVE for what must have been at least an hour. Calmly, under the speed limit, stopping at every red traffic light. For the whole ride, they did not say a word.

Sean's eyes remained focussed on his feet, not once glancing at Victor in the driver's seat next to him.

Victor arrived at his intended destination.

The police station.

Victor turned off the engine, speaking slowly, clearly, and calmly.

"I bet you want to march me in there and lock me up real bad right now, don't you?"

Sean gripped the sides of his seat with everything he had. The blood on Victor's nose had now dried, and Sean imagined adding a fresh dose. Instead, he nodded. He held his breath. His muscles strained under the tension.

"If you tell anyone about our conversations, I will kill Lily. If you tell anyone about us meeting, I will kill Lily. Do you understand?"

Sean nodded.

"I said do you understand, Sean?"

"Yes," he whispered.

"I know you have CCTV footage of me. I know you are preparing for an arrest. I know that is what you have planned today. I'm right, aren't I?"

Sean nodded. Victor raised his eyebrows and Sean responded through aggressively gritted teeth, "Yes."

"You won't find me. If you even come close, I will kill Lily. Understood?"

Sean did not nod. Instead, he shook. With fury. It took every muscle he had to restrain himself as his blood boiled.

"I will kill her in the most violating, invasive ways imaginable. Now get out."

Sean went to open the door. Victor grabbed his arm and stopped him. Sean's eyes widened as he stared at the hand on his bicep.

"Remember – disobey me and I will remove her insides, piece by piece."

Sean shoved the arm off and got out of the car. He slammed the car door so hard that the Mini rocked from side to side.

"It's time to take it back to the beginning, Sean," Victor told him through the open window.

The car sped away and Victor Crane was gone.

Sean stood in front of the station. He looked at it for a few seconds, imagining the chaos inside.

He took in a deep breath and entered.

THE HUSTLE and bustle of the Murder Investigation Room was electrifying. There was a mixture of emotions; glee upon people's faces that they had identified the killer, yet frustration they weren't any closer to an arrest.

CCTV images of Victor Crane covered the walls. Officers were bumping into each other, banging on computer keyboards, rushing around with various pictures, pinning witness testimonies on the wall. There was a new section arranged on the wall next to all the other victims with a picture of Lily in the centre.

Sean could see Jack across from him, in a separate room, sat at a desk with August behind him. August's hand propped reassuringly on Jack's shoulder. Jack's head was in his hands, his bags under his eyes heavy and his clothes unkempt.

Sean couldn't face him yet.

An officer ran up to Sean with a frantic urgency in his voice, unintentionally shouting, "Sir, sir, we've been trying to reach you! We have another body at the quarry, and a missing girl, she's –"

"Jack's daughter, I know," Sean completed the sentence with a monotone voice, not taking his eyes off Jack. "Have the Scenes of Crime Officers been yet? The Police Search Team?"

"As we speak."

"Let me have their report as soon as it comes in."

Sean backed out of the room. He couldn't deal with the chaos so soon after the night he'd had. He needed a few minutes. He stepped into the deserted waiting area, locking the door behind him and closing the blinds. Leaning his back against the door, he shut his eyes and breathed.

It's all too much… I can't deal with this…

Sean reached into his inside pocket and withdrew a whiskey bottle. He leant back, closing his eyes and taking a swig. He pictured his daughter. Focussed on the memories that kept him going. Holding hands in the park, making sand castles on the beach.

Where was she now? Somewhere with her new family, making new memories without him.

He could do with her laughter to keep him going.

Ten minutes later, Sean returned to the room of pandemonium. The commotion had escalated, if that was even possible. Sean looked over the faces in front of him, all showing high anxiety. They all knew Jack's daughter was missing. When it's one of their own, police truly band together.

Jack exited the room opposite, followed by August. He threw his mug against the wall, smashing it into pieces, glaring at Sean.

The whole room froze and looked between Jack and Sean like a tense tennis match.

"Would it kill you to answer your fucking phone?" Jack's timid exterior had worn down. Haggard, bags under his eyes, gristly, unshaven chin. His voice was of low volume; but the kind of low volume that shows when a person is truly angry.

"I dropped it in a river. Sorry." Sean's voice was soft and defensive. He knew he couldn't explain his absence to Jack. In Jack's eyes, Sean's absence was a betrayal.

Sean would see it the same way, if the tables were turned.

"My daughter. She's missing." Jack's trembling voice struggled to complete those two sentences.

"I heard."

"You heard?"

August put his arm across Jack to stop him charging toward Sean.

"I'm sorry, Jack," Sean spoke, solemnly. "I'll do whatever I need to, to help."

"We are going to the site of the dead girl and we are finding out what we can."

Sean knew this would do nothing. But, if it kept Jack occupied and avoided Victor being arrested, he would have to endure.

"Okay," Sean agreed. They departed to a patrol car in silence.

Sean did not drive with the sirens on. As much as he thought it must have infuriated Jack, he drove under the speed limit. This was going to be painful, but Sean needed to drag it out as long as possible.

Jack remained silent throughout the journey. Sean still felt the tension. Jack's hands gripped the car door and the side of the seat. His lip quivered. His breathing was deep and fast. His eyes darted around the scenery, never looking toward Sean. He was clearly doing all he could to keep it together.

Sean hesitantly arrived at the quarry. He gulped. He knew what he was going to see and he truly did not want to see it again. But, as Jack got out of the car, he could not help but follow; Jack needed his support.

Contrary to Sean's reaction, Jack did not react. He stood at the edge of the drop, looking down upon the scene. It had since been cordoned off by police tape and the Police Search Team were searching for further murder weapons.

After a long minute, Jack headed back to the car. He didn't say a word. Sean drove. Jack didn't ask where. He didn't speak. Not until Sean pulled up outside Jack's hotel.

"What are we doing here?" Jack spoke through grinding teeth. His pitch was low and his fuse was short.

"You need to go home, Jack, you're not fit to work. Get your stuff. Go to your wife."

"I'm not sitting at home whilst my daughter is still missing."

Sean sighed. He looked out the window as he rubbed his sinus. Stroking his hair back, he turned and looked at Jack. Jack didn't remove his eyes from staring directly ahead.

"You aren't going to be able to help in this state, Jack, and you know it." Sean tried using a relaxed, friendly tone, hoping not to add any more fuel to the fire. "You'll be a hindrance. I'm the best *homicide* detective –" Sean instantly regretted saying homicide as he witnessed Jack's breathing accelerate even further. "I'm the best detective on the team. I'm the bloody psychopath hunter, for Christ's sake. I'll find her."

Jack covered his face with his hands. His body jerked with his tears. Eventually, he wiped his eyes and turned to Sean.

"That girl lost her head, Sean," he reminded. "I keep having this image in my mind of my daughter. Without…"

He turned away as his words became too much. After gathering himself, he turned back.

"I've seen what this guy has done. I know what he'll be putting my little girl through right now. Even if she does survive, she'll never recover from it. She'll never have a normal…."

Sean put his hand on Jack's shoulder.

"I'll find her," Sean spoke assertively.

"The last thing that happened was her refusing to eat her tea and I told her off for it. I shouted at her. I told her to get to her room. Over something so petty, so small. And that's going to be her last memory of me. Of me shouting at her for not eating some fucking broccoli."

Sean tried desperately to think of the words to say. He couldn't. He simply looked to the floor and composed himself. He had to be strong for his partner.

"I'll find her, Jack. I promise."

Jack nodded. He got out of the car and Sean watched him slowly make his way inside the hotel.

Chapter Twenty-Three

SEAN CHECKED his watch as he entered the station. It was approaching midday.

He looked to the sky and closed his eyes. He was exasperated. He knew his team were planning to make the move on Victor. A day of trying to prevent a serial killer being arrested was not what he had signed up for.

As he entered the murder investigation room, he was taken aback by the small number of officers present. He demanded the nearest one to tell him where everyone was.

"Didn't August tell you?"

Sean threw the nearest chair, clattering it against the wall.

"Does it look like he fucking told me?"

The officer looked back at Sean, eyes wide with terror.

"He tracked down Victor Crane, they've gone to make an arrest. He discharged the rest of us to other cases."

Sean couldn't believe it.

That backstabbing prick.

August had only gone and handed Jack's daughter her death sentence.

I know how bad this is going to look. But if August arrests him, Lily dies...

Sean took the address from the officer and burst out of the room. He bumped into a few officers as he sprinted out of the station. He didn't care. There was more at stake than politeness.

With the sirens on, Sean ignored the road exit to the station and mounted the curb, cutting up mud as he drove straight over the grassy verge between his car and the road. The wheels screeched as they hit the road, Sean ignoring how many cars were needing to brake as a result.

What am I going to do? How am I going to explain this?

He punched the wheel, mulling it over again and again what he could possibly say to August that wouldn't cause his mentee's daughter's death.

With one hand, he spun around corners, as cars moved out of the way for his sirens. He was tripling the speed limit, about to stop for no one. With his other hand, he called August on his mobile.

The phone rang out. Sean got through to the voicemail.

"August! Do not arrest Victor Crane. I repeat, do not arrest Victor Crane. We cannot arrest."

He caught his breath, hanging up after adding, "Fucking don't do it" to the end of his message.

A car honked their horn at Sean as he sped through a red light. Feeling that his flashing blue lights justified his erratic driving, he considered for a moment what he would do to that driver should he have had the time to stop.

Within minutes, Sean arrived at the scene. He could see five or six officers exiting a police van with a bollard. He could also see August, approaching the house with his ASP baton in hand.

Sean brought the car to a skidding halt between the officers and the residence. He saw August mouth the words,

"What the fuck" as he turned around. This only enraged Sean further.

Sean had barely put the hand brake down as he threw his car door open and charged up the pathway to August.

"What are you doi-" August began. His sentence was cut short by Sean's pushing him out of the way.

"Stop, August, you can't do this-"

"I'm arresting a murderer –"

"Yeah, in my case. You gave me this case. We can't arrest yet."

Sean grabbed hold of August's arm and attempted to drag him away. August shoved his arm out of Sean's grasp and stood back. The officers from the van approached but August raised his hands, instructing them to wait.

Sean went to grab August again but August blocked his arms. They squared up to one another like two cats fighting over territory.

"What are you doing, Sean?" August demanded, irately perplexed.

"You can't make this arrest," Sean appealed. He turned his face to the house and cried, "Victor! Go! The police are here, get out!"

"Are you out of your mind?" August's jaw dropped.

"You – don't – know – what – is – going – on," Sean pronounced each word on its own, as patronisingly as he could.

"Explain yourself immediately," August demanded.

"I… I can't…"

"I will arrest you for assault and obstruction of police investigation-"

"I *am* the police investigation!" Sean growled at August, shaking him, praying he would just trust him.

August nodded at the officers behind Sean, who ran over.

"I have intel you don't know, I have a way in you don't know. You may have just killed his next victim yourself –"

Sean was tackled to the ground by too many men for him to stop.

"Sean," August began. "You are under arrest for assault and obstruction of police investigation. You do not have to mention anything but you do-"

"Oh, August, no..."

"You don't want to do this. We don't want to go back to the beginning, Sean."

Sean froze.

"*It's time to take it back to the beginning, Sean.*"

That's what Victor had said...

"*It's time to go back to the beginning.*"

Sean rose, elated, his eyes wide with joy.

"Stop, August – I know where he's taking Lily!"

Chapter Twenty-Four

"IT'S time to take it back to the beginning."

"So, like, back to the first girl that died?" August asked, speeding ahead. "Because that's not where we're going."

"No, August, back to where it began. This has all been about me and Alexander Shirlov. He's preparing his next taunt. Back where it began…"

August nodded. Sean's intuition was rarely wrong, even if he didn't completely understand it.

As they pulled up outside the house, familiar feelings came flooding back. It Sean had to repress them.

The familiar sight of overgrown weeds along the pavement, the smell of decaying food and the feeling of dread as the entrance of the house loomed. Sean saw himself weakly limping out of the door to cheers and cries from neighbours beneath the wailing of sirens.

The blood.

The hands.

The life of Alexander Shirlov vanishing beneath him.

He closed his eyes. Took a deep breath.

Together, they charged toward the door, only to find it

already open. They rushed into the living room and skidded to a halt.

Victor Crane looked back at them, caught in the middle of the act. His red marker was poised in his hand, the sentence of 'Remember this, Sean?' half-written on the wall. Paint cans, a step ladder, and a tool box surrounded his feet.

Victor's eyebrows raised in terror.

"Victor Crane, you are arrested on suspicion of murder," Sean declared, taking a huge amount of satisfaction.

This time he was the one looking smug.

As he read Victor his caution, August handcuffed the bastard's hands behind his back.

"Got you now," Sean added as they dragged him to the car. "Search the house for the girl," he barked at the remaining officers.

August assured Sean of his good work as they dragged Victor to the car. A horde of neighbours had turned out to watch, prompted by the police cars, accumulating outside the house. A few of them did a double take upon seeing Sean, having witnessed him leaving this house a little over a year ago.

Sean ducked Victor's head under the roof of the car and took great gratification from shoving him into the backseat. August started the engine and Sean took to the passenger seat, never taking his eyes off Victor in the rear-view mirror. By now he had come to expect the unexpected and, even though it was irrational, he didn't want to risk turning his head and giving Victor some elusive opportunity to escape custody.

Victor was grinning again.

"He's not going anywhere," August spoke under his voice to Sean.

"I know. I just don't want to risk it."

"You've done a great job. I don't know how you did it…"

"I could tell you!" Victor piped up as he watched nosy neighbours observe him being taken away. He was wearing his consistently odd outfit of braces holding up light-brown trousers over tweed shirt.

It's as if he wants to draw attention to the fact he's a freak, Sean chuckled to himself.

"Shut the fuck up, arse-hole," August spat at the rear-view mirror.

"August," came a voice over the radio. "The girl's not here. Repeat, the girl's not here."

"What did he say?" Sean gasped, turning to August, abruptly alert.

August grabbed the radio. "Repeat that please, over."

"August, the girl is not here."

Shit.

"August," Sean spoke at a low volume, completely on edge. "Victor has Lily. I thought she'd be in the house. I swear, I thought she'd be in the house."

"They will keep searching the house, she's got to be somewhere."

"They'll never find her. Think I'm that stupid?" Victor piped up.

Sean's face dropped. He wouldn't have told August and gone in the way they had if he'd had any inclination Lily wouldn't be there.

But she wasn't.

Sean's hands and legs seized. His breath caught in his throat. Whether it was his PTSD or terror, he wasn't sure.

"You're a fool. You've gone and signed her death warrant, Detective."

"No, Victor, I have enough confidence in the team that we don't need your threats hanging over us. We'll find her."

"What's he talking about?" August shot Sean a look.

"He doesn't know? Why don't you tell him?"

"Tell me what?"

"Or I could...?"

"Sean, what's he talking about?"

Sean closed his eyes and leant his head back.

All that elation he'd felt upon catching him had left, replaced by mortified fear.

"Talk about it later, August."

"Tell you what, Detective, I'll save you the trouble."

August turned the corner leading to the police station and stopped at a red traffic light. He turned to Sean, awaiting explanation.

"Well Detective Inspector Daniels, Sean and I have been talking for a while. Oh yes. We've been working together this whole time."

"We haven't been working together, August–"

"But you have been talking to him? Sean?"

Sean rubbed his eyes with his hand, trying to buy himself a moment. Trying to find a way to explain this without it painting him in a libellous light.

"He has Lily. He told me if I arrested him he'd kill her. I thought we'd find her in the house, I–"

"So you decided not to tell us?"

The lights turned green. August didn't move his gaze from Sean.

"Yes. No. I–"

"So that's what why you stopped me from entering that house? You were on the phone to him?"

"It's not the first time, either..." Victor sang from the back seat.

"Shut the fuck up!" August snapped at Victor. Someone behind him honked their horn. "And you can fuck off too!"

August turned and drove on, approaching the station, recklessly turning the corner and jolting the car to a halt.

"You see, I phoned Sean a few days ago. I told him

where two of my victims would be. I even met him last night. I took him to the site of the girl you found in the quarry and he told you nothing. He knew I had Lily then."

August's mouth dropped, his jaw hung open, his eyes glaring at Sean.

"Is this true?" August demanded, his tone of voice full of shock.

Sean closed his eyes and dropped his head.

He wished he had his medication.

August wound the window down and spoke to a detective constable coming out to meet him. "Get this arse hole in a cell," he demanded and the DC took Victor from the car and into the station. The commotion of accompanying officers went with them until August and Sean were left alone in the car park.

"I don't know what to tell you, August."

"I brought you in for your expertise and you enter contact with the killer without saying shit?"

"It's not like that—"

"Then what is it like, Sean? What the fuck is it like?"

Sean looked to August wearily. To his former colleague, his friend, a man he had so much history with.

"I need a lawyer."

Chapter Twenty-Five

THE SOLID SURFACE of the jail cell bed was far more uncomfortable than Sean had ever imagined. He had flung many a loser into these cells, but had never been given the displeasure of being flung in there himself. The sound of a water drip he couldn't find the source of grew irritating. The plain white paint of the walls was starting to peel. The potent smell of damp didn't make the moaning of drunks from nearby cells any better.

He closed his eyes and inhaled. How had he managed to land himself in this mess?

As he replayed the commotion with August, he contemplated whether there was a different way he could have played it. Questions would have led to questions, which would lead to harder questions, which were bound to lead to tougher questions still. Questions Sean would find difficult to answer.

Victor had warned Sean he did not want anyone even coming close to arresting him.

"I will kill her in the most violating, invasive ways imaginable."

Those were Victor's words, ringing around Sean's head.
But he's alone. In a cell. Surely he couldn't hurt her now…

It felt like hours that Sean lay there until a police officer came to his cell door.

"Up against the wall," the officer commanded. Sean obeyed.

The officer reached through the bars and dropped a package on the floor. With a cautious glance to Sean, he left.

Sean waited for further instructions. He received none. The officer didn't return. After a few moments, he stood away from the wall and approached the package. Slowly. Cautiously. Confused.

He picked it up with trepidation, tearing along the seal and peering inside.

A mobile phone. A note. And a key.

He took the mobile phone in one hand and read the note in the other.

UNLOCK the phone and look at the images. See what is at stake.

SHOVELLING the note into his back pocket, he unlocked the phone and scrolled through the photos.

Lily. Bound. Gagged. Wounded. Looking to the camera with eyes of a puppy about to be slaughtered.

He closed his eyes and flinched away. Before he could recoil in horror any further, the phone rang. He cautiously manoeuvred it to his ear and pressed the button displaying the green phone to receive the call.

"Hello?"

"Listen to me closely or the girl is dead," came the voice on the other end. The voice was disguised. Sean recognised the deeper pitch as that typical of a voice changing machine.

"Who is this?"

"All you need to know is that my knife is at Lily's throat. You know what that's like, don't you? To have a knife at someone's throat?"

He gripped the phone with his trembling hand.

"What do you want?"

"Use the key in the package and open the cell door."

Sean put his hand through the bars and unlocked the cell with the key left to him.

"Now what?"

"To your left, through the door and left again. Keep low. Go."

Sean walked down the corridor. Peering through a small window in the door, he observed a policeman on the phone, across the room. A few yards to the left was another door.

He silently rotated the door handle, slowly and carefully. Once the door was ajar, he snuck slowly through the gap, his eyes fixed on the back of the officer. After gently letting the door shut behind him, he tiptoed toward the door on the left.

Just as silently, he made his way through it and surveyed the room he had entered. He found himself facing another corridor of cells.

"Third cell to your right. Unlock it."

He crept down the corridor of cells, constantly peering back and forth. Once he arrived at the specified cell, he placed the key in the door.

He paused, huffing at the sight of Victor Crane. Standing with his arms folded, legs shoulder width apart, that same smug expression.

"No. No, I can't do this."

"Let him out, Sean," urged the voice on the phone. "Let him out or I kill Lily."

Shaking his head to himself with more and more vigour, he let out a long, infuriated huff.

Only a week ago he was taking photos of an adulterous husband, glad to be rid of this life.

There must be another way.

Then he recalled the picture of Lily. Bound. Desperate. A child's life hanging in the balance.

"Prove it," Sean demanded to the voice on the phone. "Prove she's still alive."

After a small amount of shuffling from the other end of the phone, a young girl's crying could be heard. "Help me, please! Please he–"

The crying stifled.

"Good enough?" returned the disguised voice.

Sean looked to the floor, closing his eyes. In a burst of aggression, he punched the cell door, not caring about the sting of his knuckles against the metal surface.

No. No. I can't do it. I can't let him go.

"Tick tock, Sean," came Victor's irritating voice.

He backed up and leant against the wall behind him.

"Hurry up, Sean," came the voice once more.

Then he had a thought.

"I just need to look at the picture one more time," he whispered through gritted teeth. "Call it motivation."

Stepping out of Victor's eye-sight, he held the phone in front of him.

He scrolled to the text message menu. He created a new message and entered Jack's number. With rapid speed, he typed:

IT'S SEAN. Track this phone's GPS. Time to get your daughter back. Bring a weapon. Do not tell police – trust me.

. . .

HE HIT send and watched the word delivered appear next to his message. With a deep breath, he returned the phone to his ear.

"Okay. Where do you want me to take him?"

"Get him a car and let him drive. He'll do the rest."

The line went dead and Sean stuck the key into the door of the cell. He turned it and let the most prolific psychopath of his generation walk free.

Chapter Twenty-Six

VICTOR JAUNTILY JOURNEYED along the motorway. Sean sat beside him in silence, refusing to look in Victor's direction.

The bastard. The smug bastard. The psychopathic, sycophantic, egotistical prick. All the ways I could kill him…

"You happy?" Sean growled.

Victor playfully smirked like an idiot had asked him a stupid question. He looked at Sean like Sean was a vagabond on the street, weakly looking up at him and asking him for change.

"Let me just ask you one question," Sean began. "Why me? Why my life you've chosen to fuck up? Why? Just… Why?"

Sean was ready for the answer to this question. He focussed his eyes on Victor, attempting to read the psychopath's tells, willing him to answer the question.

Victor's face didn't flinch.

"Answer me."

Sean was not backing down. His patience ran thin. He had alienated everyone. He turned himself into a fugitive.

He should have given Victor up the minute he'd received the first phone call.

"Why you?" Victor sat back and gazed up at the sky through his sun roof. "There are so many stars out tonight…." he muttered, presumably to incense Sean even further. "Because – why not?"

"Why not?" Sean repeated, every muscle tensing. "There are so many corrupt cops out there, bent cops, officers who actually fuck over real people. The only person I fucked over was a sex offender. So why me?"

"You are suggesting that ethics came into my decision, Sean. You are insisting that I chose you to teach you some kind of lesson about the way you live your life over other people. This is why I rise above you. Because I don't make do with this thinking. And for that, you can never understand my reasons."

Victor stopped in a car park. They sat in silence.

"Why are we waiting here? What are you planning to do now? "

Victor turned his head slowly toward his captor.

"Get out of the car."

Chapter Twenty-Seven

SEAN ENTERED the first public toilets he came to. The stench of decaying urine smacked him in the face, but he didn't care. He stared himself in the mirror. He flinched at the sight. Blood had dried and cracked to his hands.

Another person's blood had dried and cracked to his hands.

He wiped the blood off with water and cheap soap. No matter how much he scraped and scraped, it didn't work. The blood remained. He knew he needed to hurry, his detective superintendent was waiting outside.

He had just killed a man. There were going to be questions. He was going to need to give answers.

He stood still again. Considering his own eyes.

What a loser. What a liability. You fucked up everything you ever did.

A million thoughts raced around his mind, giving him a psychological punch with every image they accompanied.

Did he need to kill him? Could he have let him live? Did he need to plant the weapon?

It must have been unjust, otherwise I wouldn't have planted the gun…

He splashed another few handfuls of water over his face. He returned to his reflection, looking himself dead in the eyes.

Nothing had changed. His hands were still stained in blood. He still had the same lost look in his eyes.

That was the moment he decided he was done with it. Done with the report writing, the chasing, the hunting, the bodies, the fame, the infamy.

He would have to leave saving the day to someone else now.

Chapter Twenty-Eight

SEAN WATCHED his breath form a white cloud in front of his mouth. He rubbed his hands together and blew into them for warmth, even resorting to tucking them into his armpits. As usual, the train station was deserted. The nights were growing colder. Summer was clearly over and autumn was underway.

Victor stood next to him. Silence. Observing each other. Waiting for the other to make the first move. Waiting for one to take control of the situation.

Why has he brought me here?

"So is this where Lily is then? The train station?"

Please, Jack, tell me you tracked the GPS.

Victor did not respond.

This doesn't feel right.

A figure approached over Victor's shoulder.

Jack. Carrying a cricket bat that he tapped against his leg. He emerged out of the shadows and stood a few steps behind Victor. Confidently. Good posture, feet shoulder width apart.

Victor did not move. No acknowledgement of the presence behind him. Sean was certain Victor would have heard it, but would have chosen not to react to it.

Jack's here.

Then a thought struck Sean with instant, inescapable, paralysing clarity.

Who is the person on the other end of the phone who told me to free him?

It didn't matter. They had him. Jack was here. It was done.

"You're fucked, Victor," Sean spoke in a low, gruff voice. "We've got you from either side."

"Are you referring to your friend behind me? Jack, is it?"

Sean smirked. Victor had no escape.

"We're taking you in. Enough is enough. You gave me up, you lost all leverage on me. You may as well give Lily up now. I caught you."

"Yep, you caught me. And what did they do to you in return? Shoved you in a cell?"

"It will be nowhere near as bad as they will do to you, you fucking prick." He took extra pleasure in adding the insult.

Victor glanced over his shoulder, catching Jack's eyes, who continued to stand there plainly.

"Where is Jack's daughter?" demanded Sean. "And I'd answer, 'cause if not, he's got a cricket bat, and he ain't afraid to use it."

Victor laughed a loud, bawling laugh that bounced around the walls of the station.

"Ain't that a damn truth?" Victor guffawed.

Jack walked forward. Sean smiled.

Jack walked past Victor and toward Sean.

"What?"

Without any warning or explanation, Jack lifted the

cricket bat over his shoulder and swung it down into Sean's knee-cap.

Sean fell to the floor, howling in pain.

"What the fuck are you doing?" he cried out.

Jack didn't answer. Nor did his expression falter. He rose his bat into the air, bringing it back down onto Sean, this time into the base of his spine.

Sean fell flat out on his belly. He grabbed his back with his hands. It was throbbing violently, agonisingly retracting in and out. He closed his eyes and scrunched them to endure the anguish.

He stumbled to his knees, glancing at Victor standing a few steps away then turning his terrified stare to Jack.

"But, Jack… your daughter?" he offered weakly.

"I have no daughter," was Jack's reply.

Thwack! Jack's cricket bat landed into the base of Sean's skull. His head shook, the bones around his brain vibrating uncomfortably. Various colours appeared in his eyes and the ground he stared at grew blurry. He attempted to refocus his vision as the faded figure of Victor came closer.

Victor bent over Sean like a patronising parent would to a sulky child, looking upon Sean like the idiot Sean was.

"You think I found out everything about your investigation by myself? You think I know what I know because I'm in the station spying?" Victor shook his head and tutted sarcastically. "Tsk. You're supposed to be a legend. You're nothing more than a coward."

Victor towered over Sean, who stayed sat on his knees. He spat a mouthful of blood onto Victor's shiny black shoes.

Sean peered up at Jack. He forced his face to lose any expression. He stared numbly.

"But if you have no daughter, who is Lily?"

Victor reached into his pocket and removed a photograph of a young twelve-year-old girl. This was not the original picture he had shown Sean. Instead, the girl presented to Sean had blond hair, a sweet smile, and a faraway look in her eyes.

Sean didn't take his eyes off the photograph for a moment. The girl looked crushingly familiar.

"I found the picture I showed you off the Internet. This is Lily. But you may know her as Charlotte."

Sean drew in a large breath of air and choked on it, his eyes widening and his pupils dilating.

"You…"

"Her mother changed her name by deed poll to keep her identity away from her real father. And that father, I believe, is…"

Sean screamed so hard his throat became sore and his jaw fell momentarily out of place. He lurched forward at Victor, his hands clawing out, all his strength going into his retaliation.

"No!" He screamed so hard his voice reverberated off the walls of the station with an enormous magnitude.

A swipe from the cricket bat into Sean's spine gave him an instant spasm and he collapsed on the floor again. He closed his eyes and scrunched up his face. He was unsure as to whether he was reacting to the pain or to the knowledge that Victor had his estranged daughter held captive.

"I'm going to fucking kill you…"

Victor chortled. Jack joined in. Sean twisted his neck, twitching his lip in fury toward Jack.

"Why?"

"Because you killed my true mentor, Alexander Shirlov. He taught me everything I know." As Jack said those words, Sean gradually bowed his head, lamenting his own short-sightedness. "I wanted to destroy you. And it was a chance to learn from a god."

"I'm no god," Sean replied.

"I wasn't talking about you." Jack turned to Victor.

"You're pathetic. To think I had respect for you."

Jack crouched down next to Sean. "With all due respect, I'm not the one who just got fucked." As he stood up, he thumped the bat into Sean's cranium.

Sean fell flat on his back. Jack and Victor spun in circles above him. After a few moments, they faded to black and Sean saw nothing.

Chapter Twenty-Nine

JACK APPROACHED the house through the garden. His normal entrance to the property was through the rear; this way, if Alexander was ever apprehended, no one could pass on any recollection of his face to the police.

He paused by the back door. He held the door handle in his hand. He listened.

It was too quiet.

He cautiously pushed down on the handle and entered through the living room, checking every corner of the room. Nothing seemed out of place. Nothing seemed wrong. Then, as if on cue, he saw several children burst out of the basement to his right, accompanied by the sound of a fight coming from the kitchen.

Growling, shouting, snarling; a mixture of aggression filled the house.

He remained calm. If he was to intervene, he needed to stay calm.

He walked on the front of his feet to reduce any sound that he made, creeping along the wall toward the doorway to the kitchen.

The Art of Murder

The sounds had lost their aggression and were now taken up by suffering. Gasping for air, gulping, choking; all sounds that caused a sick feeling in the pit of Jack's stomach.

He peered around the doorway to the kitchen ever so slightly, just enough that he could see a fraction of what was going on.

He gasped. Couldn't believe it. Covering his mouth with his hands, he bestowed his eyes on the terrible sight and abruptly moved back to his hiding spot behind the door.

Did I just see that? Was that real?

As if needing to punish himself, he slowly but surely peered fractionally around the corner again. On the floor was Alexander Shirlov. His mentor. His guide. With a knife in his throat, choking for air. Jack watched as the choking ended.

Peering around the corner slightly more, he saw a man in a suit. Clearly a detective of a high rank, possibly a chief constable. Or a detective superintendent; which would be likely if they had even an inkling as to the operation he and Alexander had set up.

The police officer jumped up at lightning speed, heading toward the basement. Jack immediately backed up, moving around a corner to return to the living room, listening to every sound. He tried to build a picture of what was happening in his mind as he listened to various noises.

Moments later, he heard a quickened pace of feet upon wooden steps and the basement door bursting open. He peered around and saw a gun in the officer's hand.

He resumed his former spot, peering into the kitchen. He watched as the officer fired two bullets into the wall opposite his close companion's body and lay the gun in the dead man's hands.

He watched as the officer stared at the blood on his hands. He watched the man who had killed his closest friend, his wisest confidant. He watched the man who had planted a weapon on his mentor to give the impression that the man he cared about so much had fired shots, giving the officer due cause to stick a knife in the man's throat and watch him clamber for air before his life gave out.

The officer knelt there, staring at his hands. His hands were dripping red. Blood seeped through his fingers. He barely moved.

Eventually, the officer walked out of the front door. From his hiding spot, Jack saw the flashing of cameras, the cheering of the neighbours and the bustle of appreciative officers.

He saw the man who had killed Alexander Shirlov and plant a weapon on him receive high praise from the adoring public outside.

"You arrogant bastard…" Jack whispered to himself.

He rushed to the floor of the kitchen, assuming a position on his knees and looking upon Alexander. His tutor's eyes were wide open, but his pupils weren't dilating. His chest did not move up and down. His arms looked as if they were already becoming stiff with rigor mortis.

Knowing he hadn't much time, he bowed his head for a moment and paid his respects.

"I'm sorry, old friend…"

Seeing the team of officers approaching the door outside, he ran to the backdoor and left through the garden.

As he walked away from the house with his hood up and hands in his pockets, he swore one thing to himself. Whatever it took, whatever he had to do, wherever he had to go… he would torment this murderer. He would torture him.

He would have his revenge.

Chapter Thirty

SEAN CAME AROUND IN FLASHES.

The peeling of skin on his shins along the crooked cement.

Black.

The whirring of a flashing light overhead attempting to remain in power.

Black.

The sharp taste of blood accidentally falling down his throat and causing a cough.

Black.

Finally, his eyes opened narrowly. Enough that he could see a fraction of what was in front of him. The floor was travelling beneath him. Each of his arms were held as he was dragged along the bumpy surface. As he heard his captors speak, he decided to keep his eyes closed so that neither could tell that he had regained consciousness.

"We'll put him on the seat in the basement. I got the webcam set up there."

Webcam?

"It's time to finish this. We'll destroy him publically once and for all."

Destroy him? What were they planning?

"Once everyone sees this, they'll see what a scumbag he truly is. He'll be ruined."

"Then he'll die."

Sean stared at the roof with narrowed eyes so as not to draw attention to the fact that he was conscious. He recognised the wall, the decoration, the smell...

This is Alexander Shirlov's house... They brought me back here...

Sean heard the bang of a door opening and felt the pain of being dragged down a flight of wooden stairs. He was hauled across the cold stone floor and dumped next to a dripping pipe. His carriers let go of him long enough for him to momentarily open his eyes and glance at what was happening.

Victor and Jack. They were preparing rope beside a chair. A few metres in front of it sat a webcam. Behind the webcam was a bright light pointed at the chair. The red light of the webcam was on. It was already transmitting.

Sean frantically darted his eyes around the room, trying to identify what he could. Plaster was coming off the walls. Water was dripping from the ceiling. It was dark. It was damp. It was cold. The only window had a crack in it.

Sean became momentarily alert; the window had a crack in it! Just as Sean logically thought, he saw a fragment of broken glass on the floor beneath it. He would have to go past the glass as they dragged him to the chair.

He dropped his head back down and closed his eyes in time for one of them to come over and fetch him. Grabbing his collar, they dragged him across the floor. He felt his arms scrape against the bumps in the ground.

He opened his palm wide behind his back and... *Yes!* He grabbed a fragment of glass and held it in his palm. He enclosed it tightly, feeling it prick against his fingers. He endured the pain, making sure he had it securely and secretly.

Moments after he was put on the seat, with his hands placed through gaps in the back of the chair and tied with coarse rope behind him, they threw a bucket of freezing-cold water over him. He stirred. As if he hadn't already been awake and aware.

He feigned groggily opening his eyes and becoming shocked at the sight of a webcam between him and the two psychopaths.

"Wh–what…?" he stuttered, wearily opening his eyes, confidently giving the impression he was coming around.

Victor nodded at Jack.

Jack walked over to Sean and knelt beside him. He looked into the webcam with a smile.

"Hello, viewers." Jack presented himself like a veteran chat show host. "I would like to welcome you all to our broadcast. Especially our viewers down at the police station. Especially you, August!"

The bastard, Sean thought. *They are going to get me to admit to planting the gun. He's going to have his public revenge. Jack's going to broadcast my final moments, giving himself up as an infamous icon.*

Sean groaned. He subtly rubbed the glass against the rope binding his wrists, ensuring he did this with the smallest movement he could.

"Oh, viewers, it looks like he's coming around."

Sean groaned again, spitting out a mouthful of blood.

Jack sauntered behind the camera, whispering something in Victor's ear. Victor nodded.

Looking directly at the camera, Sean mouthed: *"I'm at the place where it all started."* He coughed to disguise the movement of his mouth from Victor and Jack.

Come on, August. You know where I am now. Come on.

"Tell us, Sean, in your final moments. Do you have anything to say?"

Sean looked up.

The sharp edge of the glass made its way through the rope.

"Perhaps a confession you would like to make about the death of Alexander Shirlov?"

He looked to the webcam. He looked to Victor. He looked to Jack.

"Fuck off."

"Oh, Sean, surely you're not going to make *us* tell them?"

The glass. The rope.

Nearly there.

"I don't have anything to say to you," he muttered, narrowing his eyes. His voice came out far weaker and croakier than he had expected.

Just bide my time. Come on, August, please tell me you got the message.

Jack grabbed hold of Sean's hair and moved his head to the side, pressing the edge of a knife against his neck.

They want a confession… They want a confession, then they'll kill me… Don't give it to them…

"I'm going to avenge what you took from me. I'm going to kill your daughter in front of you. I'm going to butcher her. Then I will give you the sweet release of death."

He flinched at the mention of his daughter.

"Yes, Sean. Confess, or I will kill her."

He turned his head and glared at the webcam. "I have something to say."

The rope fell apart in his hands. He held the glass inside his palm, keeping the rope from falling on the floor, not giving away that he was free.

Just keep them going long enough for August to get here. Stay alive for a few more minutes.

"And what, pray tell, do you have to say?" grimaced Jack, lifting the knife. "What are your dying words?"

Stall him. Come on, Sean.

"Your daughter's throat lies under a knife…"

"I killed Alexander Shirlov, and then I…"

Sean peered at Jack, who returned his gaze with a smug expectancy. Sean looked to Victor, who stood with his arms folded and a huge grin, enjoying the pain they were inflicting.

"Alexander Shirlov was…"

He looked to the webcam. He nodded at it, as if confirming this was enough.

"Yes, Sean?"

"Alexander Shirlov was…"

"Yes?"

"He was… a sick, twisted arse-hole."

Jack's mouth opened, releasing a sadistic growl as he swept the knife into Sean's cheek. Sean cried out in pain, the warm consistency of blood trickling down his neck.

It's okay. It's just a flesh wound. Keep going.

"Alexander Shirlov deserved to die. He deserved every piece of suffering he had."

Jack accompanied another growl with another swipe.

Victor abruptly threw a hand across Jack and halted him.

"Enough," Victor demanded. "It's time."

"Alexander Shirlov was a rapist and a killer! I saved the world another piece of shit wasting the tax payers' money in jail!" Sean screamed out at the top of his voice, hoping a neighbour could hear him.

Jack nodded, breathing in through his nose and out through his mouth, bracing himself.

"Goodbye, Sean."

Can't wait any longer. Sorry, August.

Without a moment's hesitation, Sean flung the broken

rope toward Jack's neck, leaping on top of him and diving him to the floor. He grabbed hold of Jack's wrist with his spare hand, smashing it upon the floor with enough force to make Jack release the knife.

Sean held the broken glass above his head, ready to swipe it down and into Jack's throat.

The image of Alexander Shirlov halted him.

Jack's face melted. Transformed.

Sean cast his eyes upon Shirlov's helpless, final look.

His dying eyes.

Clambering for air.

Sean couldn't do it. Not again.

Sean couldn't kill him.

The glass dropped from Sean's hand. His panting subsided. He fell to his back, wheezing, coughing for air.

Anxiety flooded his mind. He couldn't think.

Intrusive images of death took over his vision.

Shelley Dalel. Felicia Howard. Alison Smith.

His daughter. They had his daughter.

The basement turned to black and white. Red dripped down his vision.

He wheezed.

Get it together, Sean.

He could hear the cackling of Victor and Jack behind him. Laughing at him. Mocking his patheticness.

My meds. I need my meds.

His head furiously twitched. His hands clasped, opened, clasped, opened.

Thoughts raced. Couldn't stop.

Panic. Blood racing.

He caught his breath momentarily, thought his anxiety had gone, but lost it again.

His heart beat out of his chest like the boom of a cannon. The pace of his heart increased to the point he thought it would explode.

He blinked. Eyelids painfully fluttered.

Deal with this, Sean. You don't have your medication; you have to deal with this.

Closed his eyes. Opened them. Red vision.

He closed his eyes again and again and again, until he finally opened them and the red stopped.

He concentrated on his breathing. In through his nose and out through his mouth. In through his nose and out through his mouth.

Just keep breathing. Just keep breathing.

He concentrated on his heart-beat. Concentrated.

It slowed down. He concentrated on his breathing, allowing the beating to subside.

His opened his eyes like a shot.

He was calm. He was good.

Fuck the medication.

Victor and Jack were above him in hysterics.

He jumped up and grabbed Jack's head, slamming it into the laptop on the table before him. He slammed it twice more, then dropped Jack's unconscious body to the floor.

Sirens rung out in the distance.

August had received the message.

They were coming.

Victor sprinted up the stairs. Without giving a thought to waiting, Sean gave chase. He wasn't about to let Victor go.

He reached the top of the basement stairs and skidded to a halt in the entrance of the kitchen.

Before him was Victor, his hand gripping a knife that rested upon the throat of Sean's daughter.

Sean cast his eyes upon his beautiful daughter for the first time in six years.

He prayed it wasn't going to be the last.

Reaching his hand out cautiously, Sean attempted to retain the calmness of the situation.

"Daddy…?"

He focused on his breathing. In, out, in, out.

Tears streamed down her face. She continuously pleaded for her life. She kept on begging for her right to live.

In, out. In, out.

"Your final test, Sean. Time to choose between saving your daughter's life and catching a killer."

No. Please, not her…

Victor pulled the knife back and stuck it into the base of the girl's spine.

"No!" cried out Sean.

Victor allowed her to tumble to the floor. He turned on his heel and ran through the back door, through the garden, and within seconds, he was out of sight.

Sean held his daughter in his arms. Her eyes stared at the ceiling, foam filling her mouth, blood weighing down her clothes.

August burst through the front door, followed by numerous officers.

"*Help!*" Sean screamed with everything he had.

"Medic!" August shouted out the door. Within seconds, a group of ambulance doctors dressed all in green filled the room and the girl was carried off.

Sean was left on his knees. This time the blood on his hands was tied with his.

Chapter Thirty-One

SEAN SAT on the edge of his chair. He ran his hands back and forth through his hair. His right leg bounced up and down with agitation. After a while, he noticed his arms were shaking. He made a conscious effort to calm his panting and his shaking, but to no avail.

As the doctor entered the room, Sean stood, on edge, all of his attention focussed on the doctor.

"Well…?" Sean urged him. He wasn't used to being the one waiting to hear the news; he was normally the one delivering it.

"Mr Mallon, there is good news and there is bad news. The good news is, we have managed to save her. She is alive."

Sean let out the biggest breath his body could manage.

She's alive… She's breathing… Thank God…

He ran his hands through his hair, pacing around the room as the news sank in.

"Thank you, Doctor, thank you so much."

"Like I said, Mr Mallon, there is some bad news."

Sean halted.

"What's the bad news?"

"I'm afraid the injury she has sustained to her spine has caused permanent damage we are unlikely to be able to undo. She will be paralysed, at least from the waist down, and will likely need to live the rest of her life in a wheelchair."

Sean's legs gave way and he fell back on the chair. His eyes focussed on a spot on the floor in front of him, but all he saw in his mind were the problems his daughter was yet to face.

"Is there anyone we can call for you?"

Oh God… I hadn't even thought…

"Yes please, Doctor. You need to phone her mother."

SHE LAY on the hospital bed, the machines around her beeping steadily as she rested peacefully. Sean stood on the opposite side of the window to her room. Hours of traumatic surgery had left him tense and he didn't want to leave her alone.

The words of the doctor spun around his mind.

Even when I don't speak to her, I still put her in danger…

He bowed his head, allowing a solitary tear to slide down his cheek.

Before he knew it, the girl's mother and step-father were storming toward him. The stepfather looked concerned. The mother looked furious. She stomped on the floor heavily, led by her head, ready for war.

"This is why I said *no!*" she projected into Sean's face. "Because you *fuck* her life up. She was put in danger, again, because of *you*. You *fucking prick!*"

She shoved Sean out of the way and entered the room,

placing some flowers on the table beside her daughter, stroking some hair out of her face.

The stepfather was not so aggressive. Instead, he simply shook his head with clear disappointment and entered the room, taking his place beside his wife.

Sean watched as his daughter's stepfather placed an affectionate kiss on her forehead. His eyes welled up and he bowed his head, shaking it.

"We could have lost her... I love you so much... I love you, my darling..." he told her sleeping body with a soft voice. "I can't lose you..."

With me, she'll always be at risk.

Sean felt a tang of pain in his belly. He saw the family support she had and felt guilty.

I'm not needed in this. She has everything she needs. She has a loving father...

With one last look back, he turned on his heel and trudged out of the hospital. After all that had happened, after all he had been through, after the resulting injury to his daughter; maybe they were right.

Maybe she is better off without me.

As he stepped out of the hospital doors he found a detective constable leant against a police car, ready to escort Sean back to the station for a debrief.

The officer took out a pot of pills and handed them toward Sean.

"We found these. I think they're yours?"

Sean looked at the medication, then looked to the officer.

"It's okay, I don't need them anymore," he replied, taking his place in the passenger seat.

As he left, he watched the hospital get smaller in his rear-view mirror, his daughter with it.

Chapter Thirty-Two

FOLLOWING the debrief and the numerous psychological evaluations he had gotten used to, Sean met with August in August's office. The calm serenity of the weather outside filtered the sunlight into the office and Sean felt at peace.

August offered Sean a tumbler of whiskey. Back in the old days, they used to toast a case solved with a sip of whiskey. Sean didn't feel like he had much to celebrate, but August was insistent that, despite Victor Crane escaping, Jack's arrest itself was a success worth toasting.

After chugging back his glass and feeling the sharp sting of alcohol against the back of his throat, he sat beside August in a few moments of shared silence, thinking about August's revelations in the debrief.

They had found CCTV footage Jack had blocked; they now had stills of Jack by the crime scenes after each murder had taken place. They even had one of Jack helping to set up the various girls' murders from a few nights ago. They had CCTV footage from Sean's hotel of Jack entering his room and leaving with some newspaper clippings. Sean felt stupid, but he knew it wasn't only he who had been outwitted.

"I suppose 'sorry for arresting you' would take the piss a bit."

Sean sniggered to himself. Even after all he'd been put through, he sympathised with the situation August had been put in.

"You were a dick, man," Sean confirmed. "But I can't say that I'd have done anything different."

They shared a few moments of comfortable contemplation.

"So Jack knew Alexander Shirlov, I get that. But why Victor?"

Sean sighed. "Jack referred to Victor Crane as a god. I have no doubt Victor was the great mind of it all and Jack was his pawn, mostly because Jack didn't have the intelligence to pull that shit off. But Jack, he idolised him. And sometimes it's nice to be idolised."

"And here I was thinking that he idolised you."

Sean forced a smile. They had both been duped. Sean looked to August, who held the gaze.

"You saw it all on the webcam then?"

"Yeah…" August confirmed as they finished their drinks in unison. "Look, I know you'll never forgive me, and so you shouldn't… but you're a great officer. I don't want to lose you from my team. Do you think you'll stay on?"

Sean stood. He placed his hands in his pockets and breathed in deeply. He thought about how this case had destroyed him, everything he had lost and everything that this job and his foolish actions had cost him. Then, he thought about Victor's victims who hadn't become victims yet. He thought about how few officers had his success rate of beating serial killers. They needed him.

Then, he thought about his daughter. He thought about her being in a wheelchair for the rest of her life.

After a long, deep, breath, he turned to August. "I don't know…."

Sean peered out the window, unable to see a single cloud in the bright-blue sky. It was early morning and there was a fresh smell of dawn in the air that would normally mean the night shift was over.

"Victor Crane not only systematically destroyed my life, he took my daughter. As long as he's still out there, I'm not going to stop hunting him. Whether that is as a police officer or a vigilante, I guess, is up to you."

August smiled. He nodded. That was good enough for him. He put his hand on Sean's shoulder and returned to work.

Sean took another moment. He took a deep breath in through his nose and out through his mouth.

He had a feeling that the hard work had only just begun.

Rick Wood

REDEMPTION OF THE HOPELESS

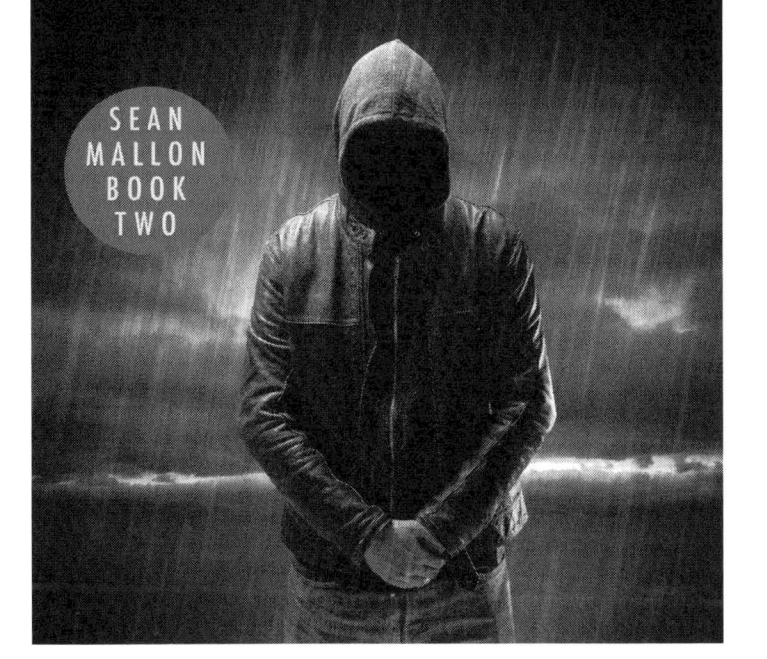

SEAN MALLON BOOK TWO

Also Available by Rick Wood

BLOOD SPLATTER BOOKS

18+

SHUTTER HOUSE

Rick Wood

BLOOD SPLATTER BOOKS

18+

This Book Is Full of BODIES

Rick Wood

WHEN LIBERTY DIES

RICK WOOD

Printed in Great Britain
by Amazon